A TOWN CALLED FURY
JUDGMENT
DAY

A TOWN CALLED FURY
JUDGMENT DAY

William W. Johnstone
with J. A. Johnstone

P

PINNACLE BOOKS
Kensington Publishing Corp.
www.kensingtonbooks.com

PINNACLE BOOKS are published by

Kensington Publishing Corp.
850 Third Avenue
New York, NY 10022

PUBLISHER'S NOTE
Following the death of William W. Johnstone, the Johnstone family is working with a carefully selected writer to organize and complete Mr. Johnstone's outlines and many unfinished manuscripts to create additional novels in all of his series like The Last Gunfighter, Mountain Man, and Eagles, among others. This novel was inspired by Mr. Johnstone's superb storytelling.

All Kensington titles, imprints, and distributed lines are available at special quantity discounts for bulk purchases for sales promotions, premiums, fund-raising, educational, or institutional use. Special book excerpts or customized printings can also be created to fit specific needs. For details, write or phone the office of the Kensington special sales manager: Kensington Publishing Corp., 850 Third Avenue, New York, NY 10022, attn: Special Sales Department; phone 1-800-221-2647.

PINNACLE BOOKS and the Pinnacle logo are Reg. U.S. Pat. & TM Off.

ISBN-13: 978-0-7860-1841-3
ISBN-10: 0-7860-1841-0

First printing: November 2007

10 9 8 7 6 5 4 3 2 1

Printed in the United States of America

1

The town of Fury sat on a large, open plain in the southwest of the territory. The land about it was mostly flat, although slightly rolling. And it was cut, north to south, by a creek—wide and deep in winter, and barely a trickle in summer. The settlers called it Fury Creek.

They had come west from Kansas City, those first settlers, and it was there that they had run across the legendary wagon master Jedediah Fury: the man for whom they had named their town, and the man who had died at the hands of the Comanche along the way.

His son carried on his legacy, however. Jason was little more than a boy when they left Kansas City, but he had taken hold like a man, shepherding the members of the train nearly to California. And once they elected him sheriff—behind his back, while he lay wounded—he had to stay, despite the strong call of higher education back East, and the promise of a career that did not include making himself the favorite target for every Apache or bandit that happened by.

And things were about to get much, much worse.

Outside the temporary Apache camp
Three hours south of Fury

Lone Wolf rode at the head of a long line of braves, each one stripped, greased, and painted: battle-ready. They were great in number. Soaring Hawk had sent all the men he could muster on Lone Wolf's promise that this time, they could not, would not fail.

And Lone Wolf was a man of his word.

They had come up the pass yesterday, ridden all through the day, and camped south and east of Fiery Hair's house. Not so close that they could be detected, but not so far away that they hadn't taken two of Fiery Hair's cattle and cooked them for an evening meal. Fiery Hair had good cattle even if he was white, and even if he was a fool.

The whites had done nothing to them. But just the fact that they existed was a thorn in Soaring Hawk's—and Lone Wolf's—side.

They would take Fiery Hair and his woman after they took the town. And they would return with many tales to tell, and many cattle and many ponies.

They would return to Soaring Hawk in honor.

Fury, Arizona Territory

Jason ducked just in time to avoid catching a slug with his face. As he scurried backward, deeper into the alley, he wiped at his cheek. His hand came away bloody and bearing ragged splinters.

He scowled.

"Damn it, Saul, you nearly got me!" he shouted before he jumped behind a stack of packing crates. For the fourth time, his hand slid toward his holstered gun; for the fourth time, he stopped himself before his fingers could curl around its butt. Saul might have temporarily gone peach-orchard crazy, but *he* didn't have to.

For a while anyway.

But if Saul took one more shot at him . . .

"Saul!" A new voice. Doc? "Saul, it's Dr. Morelli!"

Jason heaved a small sigh of relief despite himself. He'd thought everybody had taken to the hills—or at least the wagons outside the wall—a while back. At least, he'd figured the smart ones had.

"Jason? Jason, are you all right?" Morelli called. He was inside the stable and across the square, so far as Jason could figure.

"Been better," Jason called back. He touched his cheek again and pulled back, fingers dripping with fresh blood. He added, "Might be bleeding to death." That part, he added for Saul's benefit.

It seemed to have no effect, though. Another shot rang out immediately, followed by Morelli's shout: "Saul! Stop it!"

As deadly as the situation might seem, Jason had more important things on his mind, and Saul's momentary descent into madness was just one more thing to take care of. After all, Saul couldn't help it, Jason supposed. A man could scarcely be expected to deal with two children being born full-term dead inside two years. If he were Saul, Jason reasoned, he'd probably shoot up a town or two as well.

The street was quiet again, and Jason ventured forward

to the alley's mouth, a few tentative feet at a time. He showed his face at the corner, then stepped into full view.

Nothing.

No slugs sang past his ears or pierced his flesh.

Saul's wilding time was over.

Jason shouted, "Doc? I reckon he's finished."

Dr. Morelli stepped forward through the door of the livery and held up his hand to Jason, waving it. After a moment, he turned to his left and began to walk up the street while calling, "Saul? Saul, where are you, old man?"

Saul must have answered, although too softly for Jason to hear across the street, because Doc Morelli stopped, shook his head, then opened the door of the mercantile and disappeared inside.

Jason let out his breath—a part of which he hadn't known he was holding—and started back toward his office. By the time he reached the northwest corner of the square and crossed the street to the jail, he glanced back and saw Doc Morelli guiding a hunched and sobbing Saul Cohen back up to his hardware store.

Under his breath Jason muttered, "Hope Doc gives you a big dose of that sleep juice of his, Saul." He opened the door and let himself into his office. "About two days' worth."

Now, he thought as he settled down behind the desk, thumbed his hat back, and pulled open the top drawer. *Back to the important stuff.*

Along about eleven thirty, redheaded Megan Mac-Donald, sister of the town's young banker, Matt, rode through the stockade gate into Fury and made her way up the street to the sheriff's office. She seemed, to anyone watching, to be riding with a purpose—her freckled face was set with a furrowed brow, her legs were stiff in the stirrups, and she sat the saddle as if someone had sewn an iron rod into the back of her dress.

She dismounted before the office, tied her horse to the rail with a quick but decisive twist of the reins, and marched to the door.

It was open, and Jason was behind the desk, practically buried in papers. Megan let the door slam behind her and stood there, her posture just as stiff as it had been all the way into town, just as stiff as it had been since she woke, once again, to the sound of angry voices.

Jason's head lifted, but the smile didn't stay on his lips for very long. "Megan. What's wrong?"

Megan pursed her lips, then spat, "As if you didn't know!"

Jason blinked a couple of times, and looked to be carefully choosing his next words before he spoke. "Megan, I've been sort of busy this morning, and I—"

But carefully chosen or not, he didn't have much time to get the thought out, because she cut him off with a toss of her head.

"Oh, no you don't, Jason Fury. We've been over and over this. And don't pretend you don't know exactly what I'm talking about. You've got to do something about Matt and Jenny!"

Jason let out a long sigh. Matt and Jenny must be at it again, as they had been almost continually of late. He shrugged his shoulders and said, "Megan, you know I predicted this from the start. But Jenny's the one who has to decide whether or not she wants out. Either she or Matt. I've told you—and I've told Jenny—that I'm not going to meddle in their business. I haven't since they got hitched, and I won't start now."

He'd told Jenny all right, told her on her wedding day. She'd made her bed, and now she'd have to lie in it. It didn't sound like she was finding it any too comfortable either.

Megan appeared to relax just a bit. At least, part of the starch seemed to go out of her spine, and she sat down in the wooden chair opposite his before her shoulders collapsed into a dejected slouch.

He leaned across the desk, toward her, and said softly, "Megan? Megan honey, I know it's hard, believe me."

He did know, probably better than anyone else. Probably even better than Megan, even though she was Matt's sister, and even though she was living in the same house with Matt and Jenny.

But he also knew that Megan didn't believe him. In fact, she pulled back from him with a jolt, spitting, "Oh, that's so easy for you to say, Jason!" She went to her feet and all the stiffness and starch, all the ramrod straightness, was back in place.

"I can see I won't make any progress here. Excuse me. I have errands."

And she left, turning on her heel and leaving a stunned Jason to suffer the echoes of a slammed door and rattling window glass.

* * *

With Saul finally down and sleeping next to his wife upstairs, Doc Morelli quietly let himself out the front door, checking to make sure the CLOSED sign was visible before he locked the door, and pocketed the key. He'd give it back tomorrow, he guessed.

He paused momentarily, then altered his direction. *No,* he thought. *I'll just give it to the sheriff now and be done with it.*

He walked up the street in time to see Megan's dramatic exit from the office, but by the time he reached the door she'd slammed out of, she had remounted and ridden past him at a fast clip. He thought she was going to speed it up into a gallop once she passed the break in the wall that opened onto the vast prairie outside of town, but instead, she reined in next to it and tied her horse. She walked around the corner and headed toward the wagons that had parked south of the wall yesterday.

As angry as Megan looks, she's going shopping? he wondered as he reached for the sheriff's office door. He surely wouldn't want to be a vendor this morning!

He pushed down the door latch and let himself in.

"Now what?" Jason snapped before his head came up and his scowl softened into a smile. "Sorry, Doc," he added, gesturing to the empty chair on the other side of his desk.

Morelli waved one hand and dug into his pocket with the other. "No, can't stay, just had a bit of business to take care of. . . ."

His hand found the key and he stepped forward to place

it on the desk. "That's to Cohen's Hardware," he said, pointing at it. "I just got Saul put to bed."

Jason nodded. "Medicated?"

Morelli's hand went to the back of his neck and his eyes closed for a moment. "Lord! It took half a bottle just to knock him off his feet. Jason, don't hold it against him. What happened this morning, I mean. You've just got to feel sorry—"

Jason stopped him with a wave of his hand. "Don't worry about it, Doc. I forgot about it already."

Morelli nodded. Jason was wise beyond his years, he thought, then said it aloud.

Jason made no remark except to say, "Go on, Doc. Get out of here. Heck, I'll go with you," he added, shoving back his chair and standing.

Morelli smiled despite himself while Jason came around the desk to join him. It was odd, especially with Morelli being Jason's senior, but at times the doctor felt oddly the junior of the two. He supposed this had something to do with Jason's having shepherded him—and all the others in the original wagon train—clear out from Indian Territory after the death of Jason's father, Jedediah.

Still, it was rather strange.

"Hungry yet?" Jason asked. He reached around Morelli to open the door.

Morelli glanced at the office clock. A quarter to twelve. "It's a little early for me," he said, stepping out onto the boardwalk. And he was thinking, *Poor Jason! Jenny's gone, and you can surely tell it by his clothes. They're practically rags!*

"A tad early for me, too, come to think of it," Jason

replied, then tipped his hat. "See you later, Doc," he said. He turned on his heel and started down the street, toward Megan MacDonald's tethered horse and the wagons lined along the wall outside the southern entrance to Fury.

2

West of the Santa Rita Mountains
A few days east of Fury

Richard Blake, a short, stocky pilgrim with his rifle at his side and his old, worn Bible beneath his jolting seat, drove the lead wagon in the tiny train, headed west for greener pastures. His wife, Laura, sat beside him, holding their first baby, the newly born Seth. Blake felt bad about that. He had promised his wife that they'd be long settled by the time the baby came.

Laura had voiced no complaint, though, God bless her. She was a treasure. His treasure. He listened to her coo to the baby, and he smiled.

A man who had just come east from California had told him of a town not too far distant: a town called Fury. He'd said it was much smaller than Tucson, if a fellow was looking for that, and that they had most of the modern conveniences: a doctor, teachers for the children, a good well in the center of town, and so on. There was already a preacher, he'd said, but not even half the town went to hear him preach.

And after the man confided in Blake at length, Blake understood why.

So Blake was thinking that perhaps Fury was the place for him and Laura to set down some roots. He'd said nothing to either Laura or their companions, though. If Carlisle was his middle name, then Caution was his nickname.

Beside him, Laura cooed to the baby again. Blake smiled, as if she were making those burbling sounds for him. He normally rode his saddle horse, Buck, but he'd opted to drive the wagon today so as to allow Laura to devote all her time to the baby. Buck was happily tied to the rear of the wagon, following along.

The morning was clear, the horizons were empty, and the world was before him. He led the other wagons onward, westward, toward Fury.

The town had been in existence only a scant two years, built by the bare hands of pioneers where before there had only been a broad desert prairie sliced vertically by a lonely—and sporadically flowing—creek. Distant, veiled mountains rose to the south, beyond which lay Mexico. To the north, even more distant mountains lined the horizon.

Fury was the name the townsfolk had given the small settlement, in honor of the famous wagon master who had started them westward, and died before they were halfway there. If any man had deserved the honor, it had been Jedediah Fury.

Now, nearly two years since the first walls of the new buildings had risen, since Saul Cohen had begun work on what now served as the town well centering the square, and since the partially built town itself had been attacked and burned by Apaches who rode in from the south, Fury had risen from the ashes bigger and bolder than ever before.

But men had been lost to the Apaches on that day. Others had been wounded, including Jason himself, who had been appointed town sheriff while he lay injured and unable to defend himself from his "friends" in town.

Jason's life had taken a new path that day, although he could barely know the beginnings of it. He still couldn't possibly guess at the whole of it.

Since the day of the attack, the people of Fury had been busy building it back, and building it bigger and better. In the process, some people had died and others had moved on—and some had traveled south, in pursuit of a thieving gang of Mexican bandits—but enough had stayed—and been joined by new influxes of pilgrims and wanderers—that the population had nearly doubled in size, the building boom had continued, and an outer stockade-type wall now completely surrounded the town.

Those who wanted to live outside the confines of the town did so more easily than ever, since there had been no more trouble from the Apache.

Close to town anyway.

Jason had even taken care of Juan Alba and his *bandidos* last year. At least, he thought he had. Today the mail had come in, and Prescott had sent out word that a new Juan Alba, taking the place of the old one, was on the prowl. Juan Junior or something like that, Jason reasoned.

Like father, like son.

Jason gave up on trying to go west to San Francisco, on trying to go anywhere that held anything like a college. He figured to be stuck with sheriffing Fury, trapped forever as surely as an unlucky butterfly pinned to a display board.

And he was at least partially right.

He shoved himself away from his desk in disgust. Why wasn't he braver? Why couldn't he just tell the mayor and the citizens to go to hell? Why couldn't he just pack a satchel and leave like other people did? Well, some other people. On the whole, the town was actually growing. Some folks headed back East, some headed farther west, but miraculously, more rode into their little town than rode out.

And they stayed.

He shook his head and muttering, "Idiots," walked toward the first wagon.

He didn't make it, though. The mayor nearly broke Jason's nose when he unexpectedly walked straight into him while carrying a couple of two-by-fours. The mayor's lumber hit Jason in the forehead and shoulder and knocked him back a few feet, cursing.

"Oh!" cried Mayor Kendall, and reached out toward the staggering Jason, whose hand was clapped to his suddenly smarting head. "Jason, I'm so very sorry! You all right?"

Jason partially raised his head and glared at Kendall with one eye. "Been better," he growled. "What's your rush this morning?"

"I . . . I just talked to Doc Morelli. Heard about your run-in with Saul Cohen."

Jason brushed the air with his hand. "It was nothing. Doc's got him doped up and at home."

"But your cheek's cut!"

Jason had forgotten. "Probably looks worse than it is." He moved past Kendall and started down the line of wagons.

"But still . . ." the mayor said with a painful grimace.

Well, at least someone was feeling his pain, Jason thought, and forced a grin. "I'm fine, Salmon. Just gonna go down and check on our guests."

Kendall followed him out the gate. "You mean you haven't been down there yet? Take my advice, boy, and don't take your wallet along. I left with fifteen dollars worth of stuff I'll never use."

"Bet you left with a happy wife, though," Jason added.

"Well . . . true," Salmon replied, then chuckled reluctantly. "True enough, Jason." He scratched at the back of his head. "Come to think of it, most of the haul was women's stuff. You know, pickle dishes and butter plates and such. And shrimp forks! I ask you, where in tarnation does Carrie think we're gonna run across any shrimp out here?"

It was Jason's turn to chuckle. "Don't know. There aren't even any crawdads in the creek. When there's water in it, that is. Maybe you can fork yourself up some teensy-tiny little lizard eggs?"

Salmon Kendall stopped dead in his tracks. "See you later, funny man. I'm not going to offer myself up to be robbed blind again."

Jason waved a hand. "All right. See you later, Mayor Shrimpfork."

He didn't look back, but he heard Salmon mutter, "Very funny, very funny . . ." as the mayor turned and walked away, back into town. A smirking Jason made his way down the long line of Conestogas edging the outer wall of the town.

It wasn't easy. It seemed that the entire population of Fury was out here with him, some clustered in knots around the dropped and propped tailboards of wagons, the children darting in and out between the heavily loaded Conestogas. Some were deeply engaged in conversation with their mates—wives trying to talk their husbands into more shrimp forks, Jason figured—while others busily bickered with one dusty and harried salesman or another.

Jason had spoken briefly with the wagon master, an affable chap named Fred Barlow, the night before when the wagons pulled in. Barlow was more than content to park his wagons outside the wall, and seemed grateful to have found a town out here, any town. At the moment, though, Barlow was nowhere in sight.

The citizens of Fury, however, had been out in full force since the crack of dawn. Jason wouldn't be a bit surprised to find the town well draped in silver tassels and dangling shrimp forks come morning.

"Jason Fury!"

He turned toward the voice and spied Abigail Krimp, already dressed in her spangles, and carting enough loot to stagger a stevedore. She grinned widely. "I got up early to shop," she said, "and I'm so glad that I—"

"Jason!"

He turned around again, because this shout sounded urgent. And it was. Wash Keough, who to the best of Jason's knowledge was supposed to be far out of town and working his claim, came barreling toward him in a roil of hoof-raised dust.

"Wash! What are you doing—" Jason began, but Wash cut him off.

"Injuns, Jason! It's Apache, and they're comin' your way in a big hurry!"

Jason jumped out of the way to avoid Wash's lathered horse, and before he knew it, Wash had jumped down and was tugging him along and jabbering to beat the band.

"Whoa!" Jason shouted, and Wash stopped to catch his breath, dropping his reins in the process.

Jason grabbed them before Wash's horse could skitter off, and Wash bent over and hung onto his knees for dear life, as if he let go he'd fall straight over.

After a moment had passed and Wash seemed to be breathing a little easier, Jason asked, "What's the trouble, Wash? You been sippin' at some of that homemade cactus whiskey of yours?"

Wash wiped at his long mustaches and raised his head again, a look of pure disgust creeping over his craggy face.

"You deaf or somethin', boy? I just told you: Apaches, and they ain't far out of town! You gotta get these folks inside, where it's safe! You gotta man the turrets! You gotta—"

"Man the turrets?" Jason broke in.

The Reverend Milcher, standing a few feet away, let

loose with a guffaw, which he quickly stifled with his fist when Jason shot him a dirty look."

"Well, hell, boy, get some fellers up top on the wall at least!" said Wash. "And haul these wagons inside, get these critters movin'. Don't you know? All they are is Apache ladders!"

As hysterical as Wash appeared, Jason couldn't smell any mescal on him.

Quickly, he handed Wash's reins back to him and leapt to the seat of the closest wagon, standing on it to get as high as he could. He stood there a moment facing south, his back to Wash, before he whirled around and jumped to the ground.

"Hey!" he shouted, but it was lost in the crowd noise. He stuck two fingers into his mouth and whistled as loudly as he could. That worked.

Ignoring Wash's whispered "Thank God," Jason began to marshal the crowd, sending families scrambling for the gate in the town wall, sending single men running for their guns, and urging the drivers to hitch their horses in a hurry and instructing them to move with all due haste.

"Circle your wagons around the well inside the walls," he shouted. "Apache! Apache coming in fast!"

He hoped Wash was dead wrong, but the truth was that there was a dust cloud to the south, a dust cloud that was rapidly approaching Fury.

"Come on!" he shouted as he helped a small boy, dusty and crying for his mother, to his feet, then quickly hoisted him over his shoulder. "Hurry up, folks! Move it!"

3

Upon reaching the big south gate of the town, Jason ran through it and dropped the crying boy. He leapt up on Megan's horse, which was still tied to a nearby hitching post, and galloped back outside again through the stampede of men, women, children, and wagons coming swiftly toward him and the gate.

He paused only a moment to direct the first wagon driver toward the well, then spun outside the mass of the wagons to get a look at the horizon.

They were closer now. Almost close enough to make out individuals without the aid of binoculars, and through his mind raced the image of his sister, out at the MacDonald place. He prayed that she was all right, that she'd hidden, or that the braves were too intent on reaching the town and the wagons to bother with a meager homestead.

His thoughts were broken by a shouted "Jason!" coming from up the street. It was Ward Wanamaker, running toward him down the center of West Main, his gun drawn. Since Jenny had married and moved out, Ward had been renting her room. Jason believed in keeping his deputy close at hand.

"See to the wagons," Jason shouted to Ward, then wheeled his mount back across the square to Dr. Morelli's door. He didn't have to knock, let alone dismount. Morelli was hurrying out the door when he got there.

"Apache!" Jason shouted, as if that one word were the answer to every question Morelli could possibly ask.

Apparently, it was. And in reply, the doctor nodded quickly and reached back inside the door for his rifle and his medical bag. "Get your wife and kids to the center of the square," were Jason's final words before he wheeled the horse once more and headed up toward Cohen's Hardware. If those Indians made it over the wall, he didn't want the first screams to come from Olympia and Doc's kids, let alone Saul and Rachael Cohen's.

Once he skidded Megan's mount to a halt and tossed the reins around the rail, he banged at the glass out front of Salmon Kendall's Mercantile until Salmon's head appeared at the bottom of the steps. Then Jason made a sign—fingers for feathers—at the back of his head.

The mayor's expression changed immediately, and he started shouting for his wife and kids to get the heck downstairs. Jason took off for the Cohens' store, next door. He figured they were probably both out like snuffed candles, but he had to get both of them and their kids downstairs. Even with the outside wall—and the walls of their house—between them and the Apache, nobody should be upstairs right now. Jason knew what just one flaming arrow could do if it hit the right spot on a roof.

And so did Saul Cohen. If he hadn't been knocked out

on Doc Morelli's joy juice at the moment, Saul would have moved his family downstairs long ago, and be out here on the street, helping Jason.

Jason unlocked, then pushed in the front door, and raced past shelves bulging with nail kegs and ready-made hinges and bolts and screws, pushed past a display of hammers and saws and awls, and took the stairs two at a time.

"I tell you, I'm pretty sure they passed us by," Matt said from atop the ladder. His ear—attached to a head full of red hair as fiery as his sister's—was still pressed to the floorboards above him, and his attractive brow was still knotted with concentration.

Below, on the dirt floor of the hidey-hole beneath the main room of their home, sat Jenny Fury, now Jenny Mac-Donald. Her long, slender legs were crossed Indian-style, and her arms were crossed, too. She didn't answer him.

Everything about her body posture said, "No."

Actually, everything about it said, "Go to hell," but that flew past Matt's understanding. As did most everything about his wife.

Jenny had learned that he didn't care. He didn't care about much of anything that didn't concern him directly and personally and right now. His wife was not one of those things.

In a louder tone, he said, "Jenny, did you hear me? I said I'm pretty sure—"

She pursed her lips and hissed a short, "Shh!" at him. The idiot. Didn't he know they could be up there right now, one of their heathen ears pressed to the other side of that floorboard?

Her hands gripped her arms tighter, and she felt herself shiver. Oh, how she wished she'd gone into town with Megan this morning! She would have liked to have seen her brother Jason one more time, if this was indeed her day to die. . . .

Matt, now silent, came back down the ladder, unhooked the lantern, and carried it over. He sat down beside her, the lantern light washing over his hair and face before the dust kicked up by his boots rose to momentarily obscure his features. He coughed halfheartedly into his hands, then scrubbed his furrowed brow with manicured fingertips.

Jenny saw his hands tremble. He was scared. Not just scared of the Indians, scared of everything.

Perhaps even a little frightened of her.

She bit back the smile that threatened to pop out. Now was not the time for grinning like a fool. But she had suddenly realized why her husband could be—and usually was—such an ass. She supposed he was like a cur dog who snapped and growled at the person who tried to feed it. What had happened to make him so afraid?

She shook her head. It didn't matter. She supposed it didn't even matter what had spooked him so bad, probably when he was just a kid. Probably something to do with that father of his.

But it didn't matter. What mattered, right at this particular moment, was keeping him from opening that trapdoor until she was absolutely positive that the danger had passed.

And she wasn't sure.

Not yet.

Having gotten a doped and unconscious Saul and an equally drugged Rachael down the stairs and into the store's back room, Jason gave their boys firm orders to stay put and stay down, and left them all in the storeroom before he started for the saloon.

Outside, the town square rang with gunfire, and Jason was narrowly missed by an arrow, which instead of clipping him in the neck, buried itself in the side of Cohen's Hardware. The roof of Reverend Milcher's church was already afire, he noticed as he made his way along the sidewalk.

Nobody was putting that out, but he saw that Ward Wanamaker was passing buckets along a line to the roof of the livery stable, which was also ablaze. Several of the newcomers were also helping with the stable, leading animals out and hitching them across the way, north of the town square.

Somebody had best see to the church, he thought as he ducked into the saloon.

"Jason!" shrieked Abigail, peeking over the bar top.

"Down!" he shouted back, and her head disappeared behind the bar like a pond turtle's into its shell.

Rollie Biggston, the Cockney from California with whom Abigail was now in business, had vacated completely, but Gil Collins was at the window, watching the top of the wall and shooting any poor savage who managed to climb to the top. So far as Jason could tell, no Indian had yet made it over alive.

"Good man, Gil," he said as Gil picked off yet another warrior coming over the gate. Jason had always thought they should have built it higher, and now it appeared he'd been right.

"Fish in a barrel, Sheriff," Gil replied without looking around. He was busy reloading his rifle.

Jason drew and shot over Gil's head, breaking a new windowpane but picking off a warrior who'd been right behind the one Gil had hit. The body toppled backward and out of sight.

Gil muttered, "Thanks, Jason," before he brought up his rifle again and trained it on the top of the gate. "Sneaky critters, ain't they?"

"They surely are. If you're all right in here, I'm going to help with the fire at the church," Jason said. His gun was still out, but he was backing toward the door.

"Go then," Gil said, and took another shot.

Jason didn't get a chance to see who Gil was aiming at. Or whether his shot had struck its target. He just ran like the devil was after him, ran through a barrage of arrows, and all the way across the street toward the flaming corner church.

The Milcher kids had been hurried across the way by their mother, and Jason gave them a reassuring wave as he scurried past. Then the horses and wagons ringing the center well blocked his sight of them, and he was in front of the church.

Everybody was still hard at work passing buckets toward the stable, but he got Salmon Kendall's attention. "Half to the church!" he shouted over the battle noise. Salmon heard him, and directed every other man to make a second water line to the west and Milcher's church.

Muttering, "Someday that sonofagun's going to take my advice and not build that consarned thing so damned high!" Jason grabbed a full bucket from the closest man and made for the church doors.

Inside, he found that the flames hadn't worked their way down to the first floor yet, but the smoke certainly had. The Reverend Milcher was stretched out behind his pulpit, unconscious and covered with ash. An empty bucket lay beside his hand.

First things first.

Jason set down his bucket, tied his bandanna over his mouth and nose, and proceeded to drag Milcher outside. Mayor Kendall and a new face greeted him outside. Both men were carrying buckets, and Kendall had his halfway to the ground before Jason waved him off. "Second floor," he said raggedly. The smoke was getting to him, despite his efforts.

He dragged Milcher as far as he could, which was just to the other side of the circled wagons, and left him to regain consciousness in his wife's arms. He barely heard Lavinia's thankful cry of "Bless you, Jason, bless you!" as he sprinted back across the way.

The bucket line had reached the front of the church by now, and Jason arrived just in time to grab a full one from the front man, an enormous black man built like a stevedore and stripped to the waist. Jason took the bucket with a murmured "Thanks," and headed toward the stairs at the backside of the first floor.

The smoke was thick, and it stung his eyes and nose as he felt his way up the steps. He bumped into somebody on his way up—Salmon, he thought, squinting against the smoke—but he kept moving until he reached the top landing and the Milchers' living quarters.

The place was ablaze. Rugs sprouted flames like prairie sprouts grass. The sofa and chairs pocked the room like burning brush, and the heavier pieces—the breakfront and dining table and some wooden shelving—smoked in some places, flickered with infant flame in others.

Jason didn't take the time to pick a target. He simply threw his bucket of water toward the couch, barely seeing the water fly through the smoke-filled room. But he heard it hit the target with a satisfying hiss. And immediately, he turned on his heel and found his way back to the stairs.

Halfway down, he ran into someone coming up. Salmon again. Wordlessly, through the roiling smoke, he traded buckets with the mayor and started back up the steps.

Outside Fury's walls and at the top of a distant rise, Lone Wolf waited for his captains to return to him for a parley while he watched the battle.

It was not going well. In fact, it was going very poorly. The whites picked off his men from the top of their wall like his forefathers had once picked off the mighty grazing buffalo from the cover of long grass.

"I thought you said you had scouted," grumbled Juanito,

who had returned limping badly, a bullet imbedded in his thigh.

"I did," snapped Lone Wolf. "Just last week."

He had, too. All was just as he'd seen it, except for those big wagons they'd just observed hurrying to the relative safety of the inner wall. Lone Wolf knew they were freighters, daring to cart their wares across Apache land. And from past experience, he knew what they carried.

He smiled to himself. Very soon, there would be new toys for the children and pretty cloth for the women, and the Apache would all have a rich supply of cattle and pigs and flour and salt to last through the summer and winter, and new ponies.

"Your information was not very good," said another brave, his voice mingled with the cries and shrieks of battle, and of men dying.

Bobcat Who Snarls added, "It was not good, Lone Wolf. The walls are too high for such men as we. It would take men the size of gods to step over them."

"So said Raven Lids," announced the brave who rode in with Bobcat Who Snarls. The dust still rose from his shoulders in clouds. "He said, 'Then I will be that tall,' and stood on his pony. He lies where they shot him off." His tone indicated much cheating and untrustworthiness on the part of the whites.

"Pick up the dead," said Lone Wolf, "and bring them back. The wounded too. But do not stop the fight. We can win. You and you," he said, pointing first to one man, then the next, "take your men to the side of the town where earth greets the sun. Attack strongly. You, Bobcat Who Snarls, you get back to the gate."

Bobcat Who Snarls didn't look too happy, but went.

"Juanito," commanded Lone Wolf, "get yourself to the medicine man." He pointed to a brave squatted in the brush, about a stone's throw away. "Tell him I said to mend your leg before you go back to battle."

Juanito grunted, then left him, awkwardly hobbling toward the medicine man.

Lone Wolf glanced to the west. The sun was falling close to the horizon. There would not be much time left for fighting today.

Victory might have to be left for tomorrow. If this was the case, so be it.

Ward Wanamaker, the town's deputy and the man who had organized the bucket brigades once the wagons were all inside and the stockade closed up against the heathen, was busily hauling bucket after bucket up from the well.

It was no easy feat, because the water level was rapidly falling. He knew that if they didn't get these fires put out pretty quickly, they were going to have to let the fires have their way.

He didn't want that.

His back aching, Ward hauled up another bucket, handed it to the next man in line, and sent down an empty. It was halfway to its target when he felt the arrow sink into his shoulder with a sharp sting, then a burning ache.

He fell to his knees, and then face-forward into the dirt of the street.

His bucket rope was grabbed by someone, he

couldn't see who, and he heard a voice shout, "Morelli! Dr. Morelli!"

And then he felt hands dragging him out of the way while he repeated over and over, "Get me up, get me on my feet, get me up."

No one listened, not even his own body.

He passed out.

4

Rap rap rap.

Jenny looked up sharply, and Matt fairly leaped to his feet. Both remained silent, though, waiting to see if the knuckle-rapper had a blade and a spear or an arrow, or if he was friendly.

After a moment, a voice came through the floorboards.

"Mr. MacDonald? Ma'am?" Curly hissed from above. "You folks down there?"

"Yes, Curly," Matt said loud and clear. He looked relieved. Some of the color was even seeping back into his face. He climbed up the ladder, calling out, "Hang on, just got to throw this bolt. . . ."

One-handed, he slid free the four-by-four beam that secured the trapdoor, then gingerly opened it upward. Curly beamed down at them, relief coloring his freckled cheeks.

"Sure glad to find you folks all right," he said, and after making way to let Matt climb up, stuck his arm down toward Jenny.

It figured that Matthew wouldn't give her a second glance of concern, let alone a first one, Jenny thought. Had her mother ever felt this way about her father? She hoped not. And if she was wrong about her folks, she sure hoped that they'd had a nice hired man or two around. Like Curly.

He helped her up the steps, then shyly let go and took a step backward. "Thank you, Curly," she said, more for Matt's benefit than Curly's. Matt didn't even turn around, and Curly grunted nervously. At least Curly acknowledged that she was there, she thought.

Matt was at the front window. He said, "They went right past us," and then, "They're burning the town."

Jenny looked past his shoulder and saw the smoke rising up north. *Not the whole town,* she thought. *It's just the church again, like two years ago.* Jenny had been in town the last time the Apache had come. Then, they'd set the church ablaze and shot her brother. But the town hadn't had the stockade up back then. She told herself that everyone was fine and that the Apache were fighting a losing battle.

And that her brother had everything under control.

For once, she was glad that her husband didn't go into town on Saturdays.

Jason probably already had enough on his plate without Matthew elbowing his way in.

Jason was at the top of the eastern portion of the stockade, emptying his rifle at a swarm of Apache—a knot of them really—who had attempted to break through the stockade wall. Now, three of them lay dead outside it. A fourth clung to his pony's mane, his blood flowing down over the horse's withers and front legs like red war paint.

Jason raised the muzzle of his rifle and relaxed a hair as the fifth and six warriors rode away, their bloody comrade and his pony between them.

He twisted his head at the sound and creak of approaching footsteps. Dr. Morelli climbed up the ladder and stepped up to the plank that supported Jason.

"How's it going?" he asked as he hunkered down.

Jason shrugged. "I doubt anybody'll try to come in this way again for at least ten, fifteen minutes."

Morelli grinned despite himself. "It seems to me to be getting a little quieter down at the south wall."

"Don't doubt it." Quickly, Jason glanced at the western horizon. The sun was low in the sky. "Be all the way dark in about a half hour or so. How many wounded do we have?"

"Only half a dozen, unless somebody else took an arrow while I was making my way over here. Nothing serious. I think your deputy got the worst of it, but that was only because he was plenty sore already and he tensed up. Around the arrow, I mean. Took it in the back."

Jason's brow furrowed. "How's he doing?"

"Fine now. Had to dope him up to keep him down, though. You know how he is."

Jason allowed himself a little smile. It sounded like Ward. He said, "He's a tough old pelican."

"Not so old, Jason," the doctor replied as he backed off the plank and began to make his way down to the ground. "I take it you don't need me distracting you."

Jason glanced out over the stockade. The wounded brave and his escort had ridden out of sight, and the bodies on the ground lay still. He said, "Hold up, I'll go with you," and followed Morelli down to the ground.

The sounds of battle had faded away to potshots. Jason imagined the rest of the attacking force was pulling out until first light.

As he and Morelli started back toward the center of the square, he said, "Help me pick some boys to stand night watch, will you?"

Morelli nodded.

"And I don't think everybody older than I am is ready for a rocking chair."

Morelli, himself Jason's senior by several years, nodded again. "Good thing."

Against his own better judgment, Jason added, "Well, I don't." And even as the words left his lips, he knew it was a lie.

So did Morelli, who nodded again. And smiled.

"Aw, crud," Jason muttered, his head shaking.

Morelli and Jason assigned the least fatigued men to lookout posts around the stockade. The arrows had long since ceased to fly by the time they finished assigning duty for the first and second shifts, and Olympia Morelli and several other women were busy preparing a communal supper over a fire someone had built in the town square. Megan MacDonald was among them, and in spite of the scene she'd put on this morning, Jason was mightily relieved to see her there.

And to see that she was unharmed.

He had no chance to speak to her, however, because Morelli dragged him over to the sheriff's office. Ward Wanamaker was inside, in a cell, his back and shoulder swathed in bandages. He was snoring loud enough to wake the dead.

"Hope you don't mind, Jason," Morelli said, "but I put him here. The cot in the other cell's for you."

"What's wrong with my house?"

"It's full of Milchers."

Jason hiked a quizzical brow.

Morelli didn't hesitate. "I know you put the fire out, but the second floor didn't look safe to me. Actually, the steeple bell had already fallen through the ceiling, along with half the steeple. Or what was left of it. And directly onto somebody's bed. Lucky that he or she wasn't in it. And really, the first floor didn't seem any too stable either."

"And here I thought we did such a good job . . ."

"Oh, you did, you did!" Morelli declared. "But I just didn't want to take any chances. And I didn't think you'd mind. . . ."

Jason snorted softly, and shot another glance toward his snoring deputy. "No, Doc, that's fine. What about him? You give him enough dope to carry him through the night?"

Morelli nodded thoughtfully. "I think so. If he wakes, you can always whack him over the skull with the butt of your gun."

Jason laughed softly, if briefly.

* * *

The wagon train, east of Fury

"I wish to heck you'd stop yellin' 'Circle the wagons' when you wanna stop," groused Olin Whaler, who drove the second wagon, which was pulled by four massive mules, each one just as stubborn as Olin. Olin had dreams of California gold. Or silver. It didn't much matter to him.

"Why?" asked Blake.

"A body can't circle four wagons, that's why," Olin replied testily. "Maybe five, for sure six, but not four."

Blake took a deep breath. Olin had been a thorn in his side since he joined the group back in Santa Fe. "We can sort of circle them, Olin. Basically, I want everybody in a tight group. You can understand that, can't you?"

"Stop it, Rev."

Olin thought that because he was Catholic, he didn't owe Richard Blake a doggone thing, let alone the respect that Blake was fairly sure he deserved as a man of God. And which he got from everybody else.

Frankly, Blake thought he'd like to give Olin a good swat with that Bible Olin was always accusing him of thumping.

Firmly, he said, "Olin, as long as I'm in charge of this little train, we'll do things my way. And when I yell 'Circle the wagons,' I mean for you to circle them as tightly as you can. Or square them up. Whichever configuration you care to convert it to. Understand?"

Beside him, he heard Laura whisper, "Don't press your luck, darling."

He knew she meant that Olin was at least six feet three, had no respect for him, and had a bad temper, to boot. But he stood his ground. And said a silent prayer.

Dear Father in heaven, he prayed as he stared at Olin, *please get this big lummox to listen without hitting. . . .*

God must have been paying attention, because Olin angrily stared at him a moment longer, then turned on his heel and stalked off toward his wagon and his family.

"Shall Becky and I start gathering firewood?" Laura asked.

He turned away from Olin's retreating form and toward her. "Yes, that would be a good idea," he said, reaching for baby Seth as he sighed with relief. "Watch out for snakes."

"Don't forget the spiders," she added, walking off.

"And spiders," he said, chuckling a bit. He waved at Randy Mankiller, the only one of the men looking his way, to come along. Laura and Becky couldn't get enough wood by themselves. In fact, he'd be surprised if they could find any at all out here. The view to the horizon was clear in all directions. No trees, living or dead.

Randy, a lanky, part-Cherokee who originally came from northern Texas, joined him at a trot. "Whatcha need, Reverend?"

Blake grinned. "Want to help me fetch some wood, Randy?"

"Not really, but I reckon I'm game."

Blake clapped him on the back. "Just what I like to hear. The game part anyhow."

"I hear you, Reverend," Randy answered. "You think we're actually gonna find any downed trees out here?"

"Randy, I'm hoping that the Lord will provide."

The two set off across the prairie.

Fury

At eleven that night, his belly bursting with Olympia Morelli's good beef stew and biscuits, Jason finally fell asleep in the second cell despite Ward's heavy snores.

But good things never lasted long, at least so far as Jason was concerned. He was awakened at half past one by a shout and someone roughly shaking him and kicking the frame of his cot.

"What!" he snarled as he rose, aiming a punch at the kicker and shaker.

He connected with something just as his eyes came fully open to see a figure fall back into the bars of the cell with an audible grunt of pain.

He swung his legs off the side of the cot, then struck a match to reveal boots and pants. Not an Apache. He lit the lantern he'd carried inside.

When he turned up the wick, he saw Ward Wanamaker sitting on the floor opposite him, slouched forward, one arm crossed over his chest and pressed to the bandages that swathed his shoulder and back.

"Aw, crud, Ward," Jason said as he leapt to his feet and knelt beside his deputy. "You all right? Didn't know it was you."

"Didn't know it was you either," Ward breathed, his voice slurry with the last remnants of Morelli's medication. "What happened, Jason?"

"On your feet, first." Jason helped him up and around the corner and back to his own cell. Slowly, he lowered Ward to his own cot and helped him stretch out. "All right," he said. "Better?"

Ward nodded, his eyes half closed.

"What happened is that you took an arrow, and Doc patched you up. Then they moved you in here and gave you enough painkiller to make a half-grown bullock sleep for a week straight."

"Indians gone? You take care of 'em?"

"No," Jason said, and he couldn't keep the disappointment from oozing into his voice. "The night took care of 'em, but they'll be back come sunup if I'm any judge."

It was still quiet outside, but he knew it was only a brief respite from the next barrage of arrows and gunfire and the sounds of men's screams.

At least they wouldn't have the Milchers' steeple to aim at anymore.

"You send for the cavalry?" Ward asked.

Jason shook his head. "You know it'd take a week for them to get here. Either we'll all be dead by that time, or the Apache will."

Ward nodded. His eyes fluttered.

Jason said, "Get some shut-eye for now."

"You'll wake me for the next fight?"

"The minute we need you."

"Right," Ward whispered as his eyes closed.

Jason stood up quietly and went back to his own cell. As he settled back onto his cot, he whispered, "Next time, I'm gonna have to tell Morelli to give you enough for a full-grown bull."

Down at the MacDonald ranch, Jenny had insisted they sleep down in the hidden compartment beneath the living room of the house. Matt had fought her on it, but not very hard, she noted. He was asleep across the way, snugged into his blankets and softly snoring.

How nice that he could sleep.

Through the darkness, Jenny made a face at him.

Everything was quiet so far. The night was still, and she knew that Curly was secreted in the bunkhouse hidey-hole, too, along with the other hands, Carlos and Wilmer. She supposed she should feel safe, but she knew that if the Apache set fire to the place, they were locked in down here, and likely doomed.

It wasn't the most pleasant outcome, and she hoped that the Apache would ride off on the same trail they'd used to ride up to Fury. It would swing them far out to the east. Close enough that their dust cloud could be seen by anyone at the ranch, but far enough to hide her and hers from the naked Apache eye.

She hoped.

She rolled onto her side and flipped the blanket over her head, hoping to screen out Matt's snores. When that didn't work, she tried listing the things that they'd brought down with them, in hopes of saving them in case the Apache torched the house.

She hadn't been able to bring the piano, more's the pity, or her mother's breakfront. Just small things, Matthew had insisted, and in this case, he'd been right. So they'd brought along his important papers, the ones he usually kept at the bank, and the jewelry and the silverware. They had also brought plenty of water, a thunder mug, a bag filled with foodstuffs, and enough kerosene to last them through several days and nights, should it come to that.

She hoped it wouldn't, but it was best to be prepared. She had sent food, water, and kerosene to the bunkhouse with Curly, too.

Matt grunted in his sleep, and she rolled toward him. What was he saying?

He muttered it again.

Beneath her blankets, she shrugged. He sounded so happy. It was probably some girl's name, if she knew him. And she'd learned all his tricks this last nearly two years. She knew he had other women. And he knew that she knew, not that he'd ever admit it.

She stared up toward the ceiling, up toward the trap-door and the crossbar that secured it in place. *If I had half the guts my brother thinks I do,* she thought, *I'd climb up and open that door.*

But she didn't. She'd learned that long ago. If she was braver and not half so silly, she'd still be single and living in town with Jason.

With a sigh, she closed her eyes and fell slowly into a fitful sleep.

What is wrong with us? Lone Wolf asked himself as he stared around him.

All around him, braves were licking their wounds, tending their dead, speaking in low voices of the day to come. The medicine man and his potions were in heavy demand.

They had lost many ponies, too. How could they attack without ponies?

When he had last scouted the whites and their town called Fury, things had been much different.

The walls had not looked that high from a distance.

They had not been so heavily armed.

He had imagined they would give in more easily.

He had been wrong.

But he could not admit as much. The war chief could never be wrong.

5

When the sun rose the next morning, Jason was outside on the wall along with Saul Cohen. Saul was in a much better mood this morning, all things considered.

The Apache were already not only awake, but attacking the fortress Fury's citizens had made of the town. They hadn't succeeded in setting anything ablaze yet, unless you counted Gil Collins. On his way from the outhouse back to his post of yesterday, he'd caught a flaming arrow in the side.

Fortunately, somebody got him put out right away and called for the doc. Morelli started his day off by pulling the arrowhead out of Gil and treating his burns.

But the arrow hadn't sunk in deeply, and Gil was back at his post, picking off the few Apache that dared to chance climbing the gate today.

"Jason?" Saul said as he climbed up beside him. "Jason, I want to apologize for yester—" he began sheepishly.

But Jason cut him off, saying, "You were having one

hell of a rotten day, Saul. Forget it. I'm awful sorry that Rachael lost the baby."

"Thank you, Jason. But—"

"Never mind, I said," Jason replied. He turned and fired again, but failed to hit anything. Cursing softly under his breath, he crouched down and began to reload the rifle.

"Where do you want me?" Saul asked.

"Here would be good," Jason said, without looking up from his rifle's breech. "How's she feeling? Rachael, I mean."

"She will survive."

"Good. Glad to hear it."

They were outstandingly fortunate, because the wagons from which his townspeople had purchased doilies and fish forks and china dolls and the occasional guitar also contained a number of other things, including a load of ammunition.

And they were making good use of it now.

Jason brought his rifle up again just as Saul swung his rifle between the tops of the sharpened stockade logs, and an Apache fell from his pony. Dust puffed up around the body, momentarily obscuring it.

"You'd think they'd learn," Jason said flatly, and took aim.

"Learn what?" Saul asked.

Jason fired, and this time the brave he'd aimed at fell. "That bullets hurt," he replied as he took aim again.

The Apache vaulted from his pony just as Jason pulled the trigger, and he missed. How many of them were there anyway? It seemed that no matter how many they killed, they just kept coming.

As if reading his thoughts, Saul said, "How many are there?"

"Don't know," Jason replied, scowling. "I think it's a swarm, like locusts."

"It's a plague of locusts," Saul corrected him. "A swarm of flies, a plague of locusts."

"Oh."

Saul fired, and another brave fell.

"Nice shot."

"He wasn't the one I was aiming at."

Down at Jason's house, the Reverend Milcher, along with his wife, Lavinia, and their brood of children, were huddled in the kitchen. The two smallest were beneath the table, hands over their ears as if they could block out the sound of gunshots from outside.

"Samuel, can't you do something?" Lavinia asked, for not the first time.

He gave her a decidedly parental look, glowering from beneath bushy eyebrows. "I am doing something. I am protecting my family." His fist clenched more tightly around the stock of his rifle, which had been across his lap, unfired, since they rose.

"But they—"

"Hush, wife," he barked, and Lavinia—along with several of the children—gave a frightened little jump. "They'll need me more later. At present, I can do them little good, except in my prayers."

"Yes, dear," she said. She hoped she'd said it calmly. She hoped it for the children's sake. They were all a-jitter, and they'd been that way since yesterday. The only one of them who was unaffected was little Oliver— only because he was just eight months old.

"We could all use some food," her husband said.

But even Oliver knew something evil was in the air, that someone was out there doing Satan's work. He'd been fussing constantly over the last twenty-four hours, which she supposed had frayed her nerves. As if they weren't frayed enough already. Perhaps Samuel was right.

"Some lunch, Lavinia?" he repeated.

She said, "Sheriff Fury doesn't have much on hand. I think I can make soup, though."

"Fine. Soup."

From beneath the table, one of the girls said in a tiny voice, "Mama? I want to go home now, please."

Still looking straight ahead, Samuel said, "We have no home to go to."

Four of the children began to cry again.

Three were close enough for Lavinia to gather them into her arms. "Don't worry," she whispered, her lips gently pressed first to one small brow, then the other. "Hush, my darlings, don't fret. The Good Lord will provide."

By three that afternoon, Jason had finished his third tour of the perimeter. The Apache still hadn't come at them from the north, and the occasional weak assaults from the west side—the side of the stockade that ran parallel to the creek—remained just that: occasional and weak.

Jason wasn't concerned about attacks from the west. The banks of the stream were steep and still slick with the retreating water's mud. Additionally, there was no gate on that side, and therefore no specific weak point for the Apaches to attack.

But he was worried about the north. Although their losses were small compared to those they were inflicting upon the heathen horde, there seemed to be an inexhaustible supply of them, as if God had given the Apache a man-sized rubber stamp with which to create new warriors as they needed them.

Jason was just a little miffed at God for the time being.

But he'd had an idea, one he'd conjured in a moment of brilliance, and as he made his way back around to the south, he talked with the men on the wall. They were all tired, so tired, as was he, but still up for the fight. He was proud of them. He'd gathered plenty of volunteers as he made the circuit, and already a crowd—men and horses alike—was beginning to form up at the northern gate.

His townsmen might be exhausted, but they were out for blood. And they were too weakened by gun smoke and the steadily beating sun, and the sounds and smells of battle and blood, to give much of a damn for life or death anymore.

He knew just what they were feeling. He was feeling it, too.

So he gathered together those men who were willing, there at the north gate. They had their orders, and each man was mounted on his or a buddy's fastest horse. All were heavily armed and steely-nerved.

At the head of the mob, Jason looked at the kid standing at the gate's latch. He'd already freed the crossbeam. He nodded and said, "Now, Bill."

Young Bill McCallister slipped the latch and jumped atop the gate's foothold to swing it back. Suddenly, the way was clear.

Thirty armed riders burst through the gate and into the clear, fifteen of them barreling immediately to the east. Jason and the others waited until the first bunch turned south at the far eastern corner of the stockade, then kicked their own horses in the opposite direction. They turned at the corner of the stockade and rode south, along the narrow path between the outer wall and the creek bank, as if Old Scratch himself was on their tails.

They emerged into the open at the same time as the first fifteen riders and galloped toward the middle, relentlessly scattering or cutting down any Indians in their path.

The men on the wall held their fire for the moment, and Jason rode his mare, Cleo, with her reins clenched in his teeth. Both of his hands were busy with the rifle, which barked repeatedly. The riders' weapons belched sparks and smoke and bullets that spelled the end of many an Apache warrior.

The remaining Apache, taken by surprise, were easily routed.

Easily, that is, if one didn't count the losses to the town. But Jason had no time to grieve over, much less notice, the losses. The only thought on his mind—and the minds of his men—was to kill as many Apache as possible, and that they proceeded to do, mindless of the toll it took on their own ranks.

And they chased the horde away to the southeast, chased them so fast and furiously that the dust cloud raised by the Apaches' own ponies obscured the view of the meager force chasing them. They chased the Indians for ten miles before Jason said *enough*.

They stopped there, ten miles to the southeast of the town, sat there on their blowing horses, and watched the cloud of dust behind the retreating Apache grow smaller and more distant.

Somewhere behind Jason, a man muttered, "That outta hold the bastards for a while."

So softly that the words were barely audible, Jason replied, "Yeah. It better." And then he reined his mare around.

Their group had dwindled in number. Where there had once been thirty, there were now barely twenty riders, and they were all haggard and panting, and soaked through with sweat. Some were bloody. Several of them had taken arrows, but they had made it to the end. They had run the game to ground, and they were happy beneath the grime and gore that streaked them.

"C'mon. Let's get back and pick up our dead," Jason said flatly.

Someone knocked on the trapdoor, and both Matt and Jenny jumped. Then they heard Curly's voice, and Jenny relaxed.

She watched as Matt climbed up the ladder and released the bolt on the trapdoor, then threw it wide.

Curly helped him out, then sank his head down again. "It's all right, missus," he said as Jenny got to her feet and began to gather their supplies. "Sheriff Fury stopped by. Said they chased the Injuns away to the south. Don't look like they'll be back."

Smiling, she handed up two sacks of supplies, then the water bags, one at a time. "Is he still here? The sheriff, I mean." Curly held his hand down to her, and she took it, smiling. Her brother had saved them all, once again.

But Curly, after hoisting her up and letting her gain her feet on the living room floor, shook his head. "He said he had to get back to town. Had to catch up to his men, he said." Curly took off his hat for a second and bowed his head before slapping the hat back into place. "Said to give you his very best regards, ma'am."

"How kind." Her smile remained in place, but only for Curly's sake. And, she supposed, Matt's.

"How much damage to the town?" Matt asked. He had already poured himself a stiff drink, she noted.

Curly turned away from her and toward her husband. "Some," he said. "Said they burnt out the Milchers. Did damage to the livery and some of the south buildings, but they got it in hand."

Matt nodded. As if he cared. She wanted to slap his supercilious face.

"Was anyone hurt?" she asked, although she knew the answer when it came to Apaches.

Curly nodded sadly. "Said his deputy took an arrow, but

he's on the mend. Cooper, Swayze, Thorpe, and a bunch of others all dead. Got a lot more wounded, though. The wall held up fine."

She supposed he meant the stockade.

"Your sister's fine, too, Boss," Curly continued without further prodding. "Said she helped Mrs. Morelli cook up a good stew last night for the whole town."

"Just like when we were trailing out," Jenny whispered. But it didn't matter. They weren't paying any attention anyway.

Suddenly, more than anything, she wanted to see her brother. She wanted to touch his beautiful face and see for herself that he was alive. She wanted to hug Megan tight and help her and Olympia cook a stew for everybody.

She wanted to be someplace, anyplace but here. Anyplace but with Matthew.

She asked, "Curly, do you think my brother wanted us to come into town?" And immediately regretted how she'd phrased the question.

Curly said, "No, ma'am, I don't think so. Said they'd be fine, now that the Injuns have took to the hills."

Matt said, "Just the same, tomorrow's Monday. I'll be going in to the bank." He seemed to notice her for the first time. "You can come along with me if you like, Jenny."

Golly, thanks, Jenny thought, but she just nodded at him. As if she needed his permission! Without any further conversation, she picked up the food bag and lugged it into the kitchen.

6

The wagon train
Thirty miles east of Fury

Once more, Blake had called a halt to the train's progress—by calling out "Circle the wagons," much to Olin Whaler's disgust—and helped find enough wood to make a fire. Again, it wasn't much of a fire, but enough to heat up their beans and roast a few prairie hens that Randy had shot along the way.

Laura and Seth sat beside him as they enjoyed their dinner in the fading firelight. Olin, his wife Lena, and their two boys sat nearer the flames, and the two boys eyed the last of the spitted fowl. They were in their teens, fourteen and sixteen, and Blake imagined it took a great deal of food to fill them up. He supposed he'd find out for sure when Seth grew to be their age.

He said, "Randy? Would you mind if the Whaler boys polished off your last hen?"

Randy grinned and hunched his shoulders.

"Okay, boys," said Blake, and the boys descended

on that prairie hen like starving wolves on a fresh deer carcass.

A bubble of laughter broke out from across the little camp. It was Becky Mankiller, Randy's wife. "I guess riding all day must be awful tiring," she said. She was a tiny thing compared to Randy's height. Tiny compared to anything really. Blake doubted she was even five feet tall with her shoes on, but she was sharp as a tack.

The eldest Whaler boy, Thor, said, "Yes, ma'am, it is."

The younger one, Loki, nodded his agreement. His mouth was filled with prairie hen—from the wishbone, his favorite part.

"Slow down, Loki," said Laura, smiling. "You'll choke yourself."

Loki smiled and slowed his chewing.

Thor took advantage of the lull in the conversation to pipe up, "Do you suppose we'll see any Indians out here?"

It took Blake a moment to figure out that Thor was talking to him. When he did, he said, "I'm praying that we won't, Thor. They're bad business."

How strange to call a gangly redheaded boy by the name of an ancient god, he thought to himself. Thor looked no more like his imaginary namesake than that dismembered prairie hen he was eating looked like a soaring phoenix bird.

Becky and Randy Mankiller had no children, having just gotten married a few months ago, but Blake had no doubt that Becky would be a stellar mother. She reminded him a bit of his Laura, in fact.

He turned his attention back to the Whaler boys. "Why, Thor?" he asked. "Did you set your heart on—?"

"The boy just wanted to see some Indians, that's all," Olin snapped.

"I hoped you told him he was lucky that he hadn't," said Wallace Harvey. Harvey worked for the Mankillers driving their second wagon, which was filled with everything a rock-breaker might need, plus some to sell.

"None of your business, Harvey," Olin barked.

"All's I was sayin' was—" Harvey began, climbing to his feet.

"Enough, everybody," said Blake, who suddenly found himself on his feet, too.

"Richard," Laura warned softly, tugging on his pants leg.

He held up his hands. "Gentlemen, let's hold off the Indian talk for now, all right? There'll be time enough for it when we get to Fury."

He heard Randy Mankiller mutter, "He wants to see an Indian so bad, he can just look at me. Or a fourth of me anyhow."

Blake sat back down, the dust puffing up around his seat. "Enough out of you, too, Randy." He picked up his coffee cup again and took a sip.

The Apache camp

Having made sure that they were no longer being pursued, Lone Wolf had ordered his men to stop and make camp in the shelter of the low hills, far to the south of the white settlement. He was presently sitting next to a cook fire, which was circled by his best braves. The ones who remained alive, at any rate.

His losses had been much greater than he had expected.

White Hair, an older brave who had garnered his name from the silver streak that ran from the part in his hair down through one of his braids—a gift from a Mexican's firestick—spoke to him. "Lone Wolf, we cannot go home without stealing something from the whites. We will be greatly shamed."

Two of the other warriors nodded, and several grunted their agreement.

"I know that, White Hair," Lone Wolf said, a little angrily. "We stop here, take a few days to lick our wounds, then go back, stronger and better armed than before. We will steal much. We will take many cattle and horses, and we will go back with honor. Take heart, my brothers. You will see."

White Hair grunted, unconvinced.

Sneaking Coyote spoke up. "We did badly at their hands the first time. My brother, Runs Fast, was killed, and Long Tortoise, the brother of my first wife. What makes you think we will do any better the next time we meet them in battle?"

Lone Wolf ground his teeth at these questions. His men should trust him to know best. They should follow his bidding with no questions.

But he bit back his anger and said, "Because we have stopped close to a stand of trees which will make for good arrows, to shoot straight and swift and true. Because we have brought with us enough flint to make the finest arrowheads and spearheads. But most of all, because they will not be expecting us. They will not be ready. They will still be soft and licking their wounds from our first attack."

He had said it correctly, because the men around the fire seemed to relax in their new solidarity. They nodded and grunted their agreement. Good. This was how it should be. Lone Wolf was pleased.

He said, "We know now how they fight. They will continue to fight in this manner. We will make ladders to lean again their walls. We will get inside, and once we do, we will conquer."

At this statement, cheers broke out from several braves, then several more, along with nods of agreement. It seemed everyone was in accord on at least one point: that once things came to a hand-to-hand combat with the whites, the Apache would emerge overwhelmingly victorious.

Had not they proved this to be fact time and time again? It was the truth, and they all knew it.

Lone Wolf smiled to himself. "It will be good."

Fury

Jason and Dr. Morelli had chosen the part of the livery still in good shape—the part that still had a roof, that is—in which to house the wounded.

They'd moved Deputy Wanamaker there, along with Rollie Biggston, who'd taken an arrow out in the street. Gil Collins was spending his nights there, too, being treated for the burns his torso had received when he was hit by a flaming arrow.

Sometime today, Rollie had suffered much the same fate, although Jason had no idea where he'd been. At least he hadn't had a flask in his hand when he'd been hit, Jason thought. That would have been just the thing the town needed: a fat, flaming, Cockney torch. Always good for the ego.

All in all, Jason figured that there were about thirty men, perhaps thirty-two, in the stable, including the wounded they'd picked up on their way back to town. They'd lost seven men altogether, but all in all, Jason thought that they had done fairly well percentagewise.

So far.

Unlike the rest of the men, he wasn't so certain they were out of the woods. Apache were tricky, and you could always count on them to do exactly the opposite of what you expected, even if you hadn't thought of it yet.

He figured that the last thing he'd ever do was ride out and try to shoot dice with them to get them to go away. The trick might have worked with the Comanche, but with Apache, it'd be a sure and certain way to end up dead.

Or worse. Apache didn't have a sense of humor. Let alone a sense of decency.

Jason didn't want to find out what worse was.

Actually, he didn't even want to find out what dead was like. He'd seen enough of it to figure that he wouldn't like it, not one tiny little bit.

But tonight he had to convince the rest of the town to stop being so happy and cocksure of itself. He'd done a great deal of thinking on the way back to town. And he'd decided that it wasn't going to be easy.

They had only managed to chase the Apache away because they'd surprised them, and had been hidden by their own dust. The Apache hadn't known how few they were, how outnumbered.

It was a good trick and had worked once, but it wouldn't work again.

The jail door opened and Saul Cohen walked in. "Am I disturbing you?" Saul asked, his head twisted to one side. "I could come back?"

"No, no," Jason replied, waving his hands. Saul was already halfway out the door, but stopped. "What can I do for you, Saul?"

Saul came back in, although his posture was more like that of a beaten dog than the town's hardware store owner and an upstanding citizen. He plopped down in the wooden chair opposite the desk.

"What?" Jason repeated, perhaps a bit more sharply than he intended. It had been a long day. "Sorry, Saul. Don't mind me. I'm about used up."

"That's what I was afraid of."

Jason frowned, but it was brief. Maybe Saul was feeling the same worries he was. He hoisted one brow. "What you getting at, Saul?"

"I'm not so sure those Apache are done with us, Jason. Now, don't go believing that I'm a millstone around everybody's neck, or that I'm making like the boy who cried 'Wolf!' It's just that—"

"Whoa up there," Jason said with a wave of his hands. "You're thinking right, Saul. I don't think this thing is done yet either."

Saul, looking relieved, nodded his agreement.

"Never say, 'I expect' when you're talking about Apache. But having said that," Jason added with a grin, "I'd say we could expect them back any day now."

"They're just regrouping?"

Jason nodded. "We've got to be ready for the next onslaught. And I mean more than ready."

"So what do we do?"

"Other than getting everybody to stop celebrating?" Jason said.

Saul shook his head sadly. "Salmon Kendall is making a speech."

"Crud."

Both men fell into silence.

After five long minutes, Jason stood up.

Saul, startled, suddenly looked hopeful. "You have it?"

Jason walked across the room, toward the potbellied stove, and lifted the coffeepot. "Only if you mean the coffee. Want some?"

Saul shrugged. "I could drink."

Jason grunted, then poured out two cups. He handed Saul one, then returned to his chair. He didn't drink, though. He kept turning the metal cup in his hands, around and around, and staring at the mottled blue enamel.

"Does that help for thinking?"

Jason put the cup down. "Not really."

"Oh."

Jason kept pushing the cup around with his index finger, still staring down at its steaming black-brown contents. Steam. He thought it looked like smoke rising from the cup.

And then, quite suddenly, something went "click"

inside his brain. He gripped the front of the desk. "Saul!" he shouted, and poor Saul jumped. "Aren't those wagons carrying oil?"

"Y-yes," Saul answered, still wondering if Jason had lost his mind. "A whole wagon full of whale oil, and half a load of kerosene, too. That's why we piled all that lumber over the top of it, remember? Why? Is your lamp running low?"

Jason hopped to his feet and grabbed his hat off the rack. "C'mon, c'mon," he urged, waving a hand toward the door. "We've got to start everybody digging!"

Saul took a swig of his coffee. "Digging?"

"Yes, yes!" Jason half-shouted. "We've got to dig a whatchacall! A moat!"

Saul still didn't understand it, but here it was, after midnight, and he was shoveling hard chunks of caliche shoulder to shoulder with Mayor Kendall and Colorado Gooding, digging a ditch about ten feet from the stockade and parallel to it, and digging it three feet deep and six feet across. Jason's orders.

He hadn't said anything, but Saul was beginning to have his doubts about Jason. Did he intend to fill this "moat" with water? Did he think it would stop the Apache for a second? But he kept shoveling just the same.

And shoveling wasn't easy. The ground was hard caliche soil—the crust of it was anyway—and he figured they could have built a castle out of the top blocks they were cutting. Jason was having them pile the caliche into a wall on the stockade side of the moat.

Just how this would protect them was beyond Saul. It was beyond Colorado, too. He didn't say much, but every once in a while, Saul could hear him mumble, "Boy's crazy as a loon!"

Salmon was of much the same mind. "What the heck are we digging this thing for?" he'd asked Saul, over and over. "You'd think he'd confide in the mayor!"

Saul imagined that all the men, stretching down the wall, shovels working, were of much the same curious mind. It would have helped a great deal if Jason had given him—or someone, anyone!—an idea of what was going on in that flaxen head of his.

But he hadn't, and now here they were, digging a moat by lamplight.

He thought back over their conversation—the part before Jason put them all to digging. Jason had asked him about the oil, hadn't he? But what good would that do? A wagonload wasn't enough to fill this blasted moat they were digging. And besides, the dry, thirsty ground would drink that measly load of oil straight off.

He had a sudden vision of them pouring barrel after barrel of water on the ground, which acted like a giant sponge, and he shuddered.

"What's'a matter with you?" Colorado asked from beside him, to the right. "You look like you just seen a ghost."

"It's nothing," Saul said, and hustled himself back to digging. "Nothing at all."

Jason was on the northern side of the stockade with about twenty men, and they were performing the same duties as the men to the south. He'd put extra men on the south, because that was the side the Apache would likely attack first. Jason might not even need a trench to the north, but he wasn't about to take any chances.

He dug like the devil himself was on his tail, dug like his life depended on it—because he figured it did. He'd had words with the driver of the oil wagon after he gave orders and put Saul and the others to work.

The driver thought that the oil would soak in, all right, but that enough would stay near the surface that it would burn. And burn for a long time, according to the train's wagon master, Fred Barlow. He'd said, "Oil don't soak in near so fast as water." Especially if there was clay down there under the caliche to block its soaking in any further.

And there was clay.

At least, he remembered that Saul had hit about ten feet of it when he was digging the well. Jason hoped the soil was the same outside the town walls. He'd staked all their lives on it, in fact.

Don't think about it, he told himself. *Just dig. Just dig.*

One half mile from the town's southern wall, an Indian pony stopped and its rider slipped artfully to the ground. Hunching low, even though there was no one there to see him, Strangles Coyotes scurried to a clump of brush and stretched out low, his belly pressed to the ground.

Strangles Coyotes's eyes were already accustomed to the dark because he'd been riding for hours, riding back up north from the place where his people had stopped. And so he could see through the night as well as a man could. Better than most, in fact. The moon was full, the sky bereft of clouds.

And what he saw to the north disturbed him, although he couldn't say why. White men were doing what they usually did, which was to act crazy.

Maybe thirty of them were outside the wall on the south side. They had carried lamps like small campfires with them, and they were digging, digging like fools. At first, he thought that perhaps they were going to bury their dead in the long trench, but then he realized that the grave was far too big to hold their dead, even using the most optimistic count.

It was a great puzzle and he wished, for a moment, that Lone Wolf had sent Toad That Hops or Dream Stirrer instead of him. Someone who had more insight into the mysteries of the whites than he had. Someone who could understand what they were up to.

It was beyond him.

He leaned to one side and flicked a sharp rock from beneath his chest, and then went back to puzzling over what those crazy whites were doing.

7

Jason, having gone to sleep at three in the morning, was up by five. But when there was no sign of an Apache attack by seven, he had the north gate opened and two wagons driven out beyond the stockade. Moving slowly, he oversaw the unloading of barrel after barrel of whale oil until they had gone around the entire town and come around to the south gate.

While the men poured out the whale oil sparingly into the ditch, Jason and a few more men took the kerosene around the same way, but they didn't empty those smaller kegs. Instead, they put them down in the ditch, a sealing board cracked and broken in the top of each—not wide enough to allow too much evaporation, but enough that a flame could reach the contents and set them afire. He affixed a long wick to each—long enough to reach from the keg to the top of the wall.

"There's probably a better way to do this," he muttered to Saul, "but I can't think of what it is."

Saul, obviously far more confused than Jason, just blinked and nodded.

Jason reined the team back through the gate to rejoin the wagon that had gone before them and distributed the casks of whale oil. The wagon rattled and bumped along, and Jason said, "Lighter load."

"By far," replied Saul. The wagon was empty.

Jason was too relieved to have dug his ditch and put the oil and kerosene in place to pay much attention to Saul's unease. He chalked it up to an understandable nervousness over what was to come. He just hoped that Saul wouldn't go out of his head again and chase him around the square with a loaded gun.

He hadn't much cared for that.

"What time you got?" he asked.

Saul dipped fingers into his pocket, pulled out his watch, then flipped the case open. "Nine. Seven after, if you're wanting I should be precise."

Jason nodded. After nine, and still no Apache. Not a single, solitary brave. Maybe they had run them off for good. Or maybe they were still out there, lurking or plotting. Or something.

He pulled the wagon back into the circle around the well and said, "That's that."

Saul didn't say anything, he just climbed down. Jason followed suit. A couple of the men from the sales train ran to unhitch the horses, and Jason started for the front gate, which a carriage had just come through. Jenny and Matt stepped out of the carriage.

Jason's initial glee turned to annoyance at the sight of Matt. But he walked toward them anyway. He could put up with Matt for a second or two for a chance to see his sister here in town, and away from that damn ranch of Matt's.

Jenny saw him coming, and broke away from Matt to run to Jason. She fairly leapt into his arms and began to sob into his chest.

It wasn't like Jenny, not at all, and at first Jason thought she was hurt. But then he glanced up at Matt and saw the look of annoyance on his face, and realized she'd either had a good scare or a good fight with Matt. Both possibilities left him angry.

He didn't say anything, though. He just tucked Jenny's shoulders beneath his arm and slowly led her back to the office. He would have taken her home, but their house was likely still chock full of Milchers. He hadn't seen any of them yet this morning, and he didn't imagine it would do Jenny any good to spend a morning with them. At any time, let alone today.

Saul watched Jason lead his sister to the jail, and suddenly remembered that he had folks to check on, too. He made his way over to the hardware store and let himself in. Rachael and the boys were still where he'd left them—in the back room on the first floor. Nobody was going upstairs until this Apache trouble was over for certain, and if Jason expected more trouble, Saul was the first to agree with him.

He had known Jason long enough and seen him in action enough times to trust him with his life, and those of his family.

Even if he wasn't Jewish.

But then, Jason couldn't help that, could he? A man was what he was born to be.

"Rachael, my love," he said softly. "How are you feeling this morning?"

"Lonely. Lost." She patted the quilt next to her on the little bed. "Sit, Saul. I'm better."

When he sat next to her, she took his arm and asked more quietly, "How goes it out there?" She nodded toward the street.

"It goes well," he said. "Jason is on the job."

"And what of the Indians? The boys told me some of it."

When? She had been unconscious or sleeping every time he had been with her. At first he didn't know whether he should be cross with the boys, but he decided not. Indians were a great excitement to them still, and who better to share their excitement with than their beloved mother? Especially since their father was busy outside.

"Yes," he said, "I suppose they could not keep it to themselves. Although," he added, turning to them, "we need to discuss what they were doing out front, by the windows."

The youngest ducked behind the old, broken rocking chair and covered his backside, locking his hands behind him.

"Later," Saul added, and tried to keep the laughter from his voice.

He felt a tug at his sleeve and turned back to Rachael. "What is Jason doing?" she asked.

Saul shrugged. "He had us up half the night, digging

a shallow moat—that's what he called it, a moat—around the town. And first thing this morning, he had us drizzle whale oil and put kerosene kegs in it. I think he plans to set it afire when the Apache attack again, but I can't see how it will do any good. The soil—if one can call it that—soaked up the oil the moment we poured it in, and the kerosene he had us leave in the kegs."

Rachael's face screwed up, and he knew she was deep in thought. Not so deep, he hoped, that she would misunderstand the foolishness of Jason's ploy.

But quite suddenly, her face lit up. "Yes, Saul, yes, I see. We are lucky to have such a wise sheriff!"

Wise?

Was this his Rachael speaking, she who saw through him every time, she who always knew what was best?

He stared at her curiously, and she said, "Oh, Saul, don't you see? Don't you remember the time you burnt down my father's storage shed?"

He nodded. One match! One match dropped ten feet from the building, only smoking, and *whoosh!* "Why do you bring this up now, woman?" It must have happened ten years ago!

She rolled her eyes. "Because, my poor, dear Saul, the place where you dropped your match was the place where my mother used to pour out her old cooking oil!"

Still, he didn't understand, and she continued. "The oil stays in the ground for many years. It is like . . . a wick. A dirt wick, if there is such a thing. That is why they had such a hard time putting it out."

Suddenly, realization—as well as relief—washed over Saul. "Aha!" he said. "Once again, our boy sheriff is three steps ahead of me. But not you, Rachael," he added with a self-effacing grin. "No, not ahead of my Rachael."

"I hate him, Jason," Jenny said, hunched over with her hands to her eyes. "I wanted the Apache to come and kill him, even if they killed me, too!" And then she burst back into uncontrollable tears.

Jason held a cup of water to her trembling lips. "Here, Jenny. Drink this."

But she pushed the cup away, splashing water over her lap and his, and she couldn't stop crying.

So he just held her. He hadn't wanted it to happen like this, but he had wanted her to leave Matt and to come home. She needed to grow up. And she needed somebody besides Matt MacDonald to do it with. Someone besides her husband.

But she'd thrown Jason out of the mix when she married Matt. It was against everything he'd ever been taught, breaking up a marriage. Especially his own sister's. He tried to think like his father. What would Jedediah Fury have done?

Jedediah wouldn't have allowed Jenny to run off with Matt in the first place, that's what, Jason thought with a frown. Never, not in a million years would he have allowed his only daughter to wed such a cowardly little pissant as Matthew MacDonald. Well, Jason hadn't exactly allowed it either, but the Reverend Milcher had wed them just the same. And now Matt was his brother-in-law.

Jenny spoke. "Jason, I want to come home. And not just to visit. To stay."

"Are you absolutely sure, Jenny?" he asked, holding his sudden joy from his voice. He didn't want her to go through this a second time. He didn't think he could stand it, and he knew that she couldn't.

"Yes," she said through her tears. "I'm positive."

Not unkindly, Jason said, "You were positive you wanted to marry him, too, Jen."

She lifted her head to face him, and her expression was hard and determined. "I know. I was wrong. I should have listened to you."

Jason blinked. He hadn't expected that—her saying that she should have listened to him, that is. He knew how hard that must have been for Jenny, and he softened.

"Of course you can come back, honey," he said, and gave her a brotherly hug. "Of course you can. But you'll have to stay with me here for a while. Our house is full of Milchers."

She blinked. "Why on earth?"

"Didn't you see the church when you came through the gate?"

Jenny blew her nose. "Wasn't paying attention."

"They got burnt out, from the steeple down to the ground."

"Oh," Jenny sniffed. "All right. I'd like to stay here with you. Is . . . is Megan here in town still?"

Jason nodded. "She's around. Or she was, last time I checked. You can go look for her, but if you hear anybody shout 'Apache,' you head back here in a hurry, you understand me?"

She bobbed her head like a dutiful sister, and he smiled before he said, "We're not out of this thing yet, baby sister. Keep close."

He stood up and started toward the door, but she said, "Jason? Why didn't you stay to talk to me when you came by the house yesterday?"

He couldn't answer her, couldn't tell her that he would just as soon slug her husband in the face as speak to him. And so he simply walked out the door without answering.

Once outside, he walked right into Megan. She fell back into the hitching rail, and only fast thinking on Jason's part kept her from going over it backward.

"Sorry," he said as he brought her back to her feet with as little show as possible.

Her feathers were ruffled, though, and while she smoothed her skirts, she started to scold him.

He waved his hands, saying, "Megan? Megan!"

She stopped her rant and stared at him curiously. "What?"

"Jenny's inside. She wants to talk to you."

"And I want to talk to her, too," Megan said, and pushed past him to the office door.

"Take it easy on her, Megan. Please? And tell her I've been taking good care of her filly."

She looked at him, her face relaxing as she did. "All right, Jason. She'll be happy to hear about Nugget. Did she have a rough time of it? Jenny, not Nugget, I mean."

"I'm guessing she did, but it didn't have anything to do with the Apache."

"I didn't think so," she said cryptically, and disappeared into the office, closing the door softly behind her.

"There was nothing more?" Lone Wolf asked. It was nearing noon at the Apache camp, and he had spent the morning questioning Strangles Coyotes about what he'd seen at the whites' town. So far, he wasn't getting any information, at least none that did him any good.

"Nothing," said Strangles Coyotes. He was so tired that his head was wobbling on his neck and his eyelids fluttered. He had started back before dawn, long before light, long before Jason had begun to implement the second part of his plan.

"They dug a ditch," said Lone Wolf. "They are crazy, these whites."

Strangles Coyotes gave a halfhearted nod. "Crazy," he repeated.

Lone Wolf had had enough of him. "Go. Sleep. And when you wake, make arrows. Many arrows. We will need them tomorrow."

"We attack again in the morning?"

Lone Wolf nodded curtly. "Go and sleep. We need each man at his best."

At last, Strangles Coyotes left and Lone Wolf fell once again into thought. What could the whites be planning to dig this ditch? The Apache ponies would not stumble in it. They were all surer of foot, more nimble, than the mountain goats.

Perhaps the whites intended to divert the stream into it. But again, what good would that do them? It would only be a waste of water, and according to Strangles Coyotes, it was now shallow enough to be easily forded. Even when it was at its raging height, the river still did not meet the tops of the bank, let alone the height of the ditch. He did not think even the craftiest white could make water run uphill.

Slowly, he shook his head. Whatever they were planning, his braves would overcome. Tomorrow they would spread themselves around the whole of the wall's perimeter.

Tomorrow, they would be victorious, and two days later, they would celebrate their victory with the rest of the tribe. There would be much feasting on the white men's cattle and drinking of tiswin and dancing.

He was sure of it.

The whites were many in number and had firesticks with which to shoot them, but they were as stupid as women when it came to planning. They would fail, and his men would sack and strip the town.

Of this, he was certain.

8

The wagon train

Randy Mankiller sat down next to his wife with a *thump*.

"Finished?" she asked.

"Yeah, all done," he replied. The Whalers' wagon had hit a rock and broken an axle early in the morning, and it had taken half a day to unload it so it could be blocked up, and then the other half to fit the axle—thank goodness that old crank, Olin, had brought a spare!—get it back down on the ground, and load it back up again.

Altogether, he figured they'd made about twenty-five feet of travel for the entire day.

He guessed he must have looked plenty disgusted, because suddenly, he felt a small, cool hand on the back of his neck, then felt it begin to gently knead the muscles there.

"Good," he said, closing his eyes. "That's awful good, honey."

He heard the rustle of her skirts as she moved behind him, then felt a second hand join the first. Their movements, although still gentle, became firmer, and Randy groaned with pleasure.

"Feeling better, I take it?" came Becky's voice from behind him. "You're making those *yummy* sounds again. You know, like the ones you made last night, when we made—"

"Hush, honey!" he said, twisting around. "Somebody'll hear!"

She giggled, but kept rubbing his neck. "My big ol' worrywart," she said with a smile. "Nobody can hear us. They're all either too far away or they're asleep."

Randy, who had eased back around and lowered his head, opened his eyes. "Not me," he said.

"Of course not you," Becky soothed, a hint of a smile in her voice.

"Tomorrow will be better," he mumbled. Sleep was trying to overtake him. "It will. We'll make it up tomorrow."

"Of course we will," she said. "You just relax for now. You deserve it."

"Deserve it," he thought he echoed.

"That's my boy," she said, although it sounded like she was very far away. "Just sleep, just sleep . . ."

When night fell, the Milchers were back in their own house—the town had pitched in to make the second floor habitable again, although it was barely that—and Jenny was back at Jason's home and sharing a room with Megan, who was still too mad at everybody and everything to go to her own ranch. Jason was planning on camping out at the jail again. He would much rather have spent the night with the girls.

At least he had eaten with them. Jenny, who alternately beamed and laughed or burst into tears for no particular reason, had fried a chicken, and Megan had looted their overgrown garden for the greens to make a salad, peas to steam or boil, and new potatoes to bake with cheese.

Aside from Jenny's occasional bouts of tears, it had been the best meal he'd had in a long time.

Well, the chicken was a little burned, but it still tasted great.

Now, as he patrolled the streets for the last time, nodding to the odd townsman still up and listening to the hum of drowsy conversation from the wagons circled around the well, he almost began to feel as if things might be all right again.

Almost.

There were still a few things wrong. The Apache, for instance. And the fact that at the moment, he had Matt MacDonald locked up back at the jail.

He was sort of hoping to walk around until Matt fell asleep, as a matter of fact.

He checked his pocket watch. It was a quarter till midnight. He sighed. He guessed it was time he turned in. He could always just shoot Matt, he supposed. He grinned at the thought of it, and opened the door to the jail.

It was darker inside than out, with no sound to be heard except for Matt's snores. Good. He was in luck. Lighting a lantern, he turned the flame low and proceeded to the spare cell. He took his boots off, set his hat aside, stretched out on the cot, and blew out the lantern. Matt didn't stir through any of it.

Jason closed his eyes and fell asleep almost before his lashes touched his cheeks.

At about three in the morning, Ward Wanamaker, over at the stable-cum-hospital, woke and felt as lively as he had ever felt in all his life. Well, except for his arm and shoulder, that is. But even that felt a whole lot better than it had before he fell asleep. Whenever that had been.

But everybody around him was sleeping. He figured he'd go over to the jail and try to make himself useful, or maybe find someone to talk to, anyway. He stood up and started for the stable door, wincing when he accidentally rubbed his shoulder on the edge of the doorway.

"Jeez," he muttered beneath his breath. He gripped his shoulder and went on.

He found the jail dark once he rounded the well and its circle of wagons, and he opened the door thinking that he'd have the place to himself. But then somebody snored. Loudly.

The lantern had been moved, but he felt his way to the desk and grabbed a candle and a match from the top drawer. The candle lit, he held it aloft and peered into the cells.

"Jason?" he said, quite a bit more loudly than he needed to.

"Mmm . . . what? What?" Jason leapt to his feet, tripped over his boots, and barely caught himself on the bars. "Aw, crud, Ward! What the hell are you doing over here?"

In the cell behind Jason's, another body—Matt's— stirred, but neither Jason nor Ward paid it much mind.

"In case you forgot, this is where I work," Ward said.

Jason was squinting at the wall clock. "At three in the morning?"

Ward bit at his lower lip. "Uh, night shift?"

"What's going on?" mumbled the occupant of the second cell.

Ward held his candle higher. "Matt? What in tarnation are you doin' here?"

"Shut up, the both of you!" Jason said.

Matt, who had started to stand up, sat back down with a thump, stretched out, and pulled the blanket over his head.

Jason sat down to pull on his boots and Ward asked, "What's Matt doin' in here? Did he stick up his own bank or somethin'?"

Jason snorted, but he smiled. "Naw, the jackass was going to go home right at dusk. Trying to ride home in that carriage, big as life."

From beneath his blanket, Matt said, "I was perfectly safe, Fury. I had a rifle under the seat and—"

"Shut up," Jason said again, and stood up, his boots on his feet and his hat on his head. "Now that I'm awake, I'm awake. Thank you, Ward."

Ward scratched at the back of his head. "Sorry, Jason."

"It's done," said Jason. "I'm going to check the town again."

"Why?"

One hand on the door latch, Jason stopped stock still and stared at him. "Why? Why should I check my town when it's done nothing but fend off Apache for the last couple of days? Well, all right, not today, but that's just a lull in the proceedings. I fully expect—"

Ward held up his free hand. "Go. But first, where'd you hide the dang lamp?"

Jason opened the door. "In my cell," he said as he closed it behind him.

Shrugging, Ward went to the first cell and retrieved the lamp. As he headed back toward the desk, he heard Matt's voice, still muffled by the blanket, say, "He's crazy, you know. Those Apache aren't going to attack us again."

Ward sat down behind the desk and applied the lit candlewick to the lantern, then turned up the flame. "You know that for sure, Matt?"

In the dim light, Matt lowered his blanket and scowled. "No, genius. I just have the common sense I was born with. Those Indians were scared. They're beaten. They're gone for good."

Ward said, "Uh-huh," and opened the newest seed catalogue. "You figure that out while we was gettin' shot fulla arrows and scalped—"

Matt interjected, "Apache don't scalp, you moron."

"—and such here in town?" Ward went on, oblivious. "You put the fear of God into 'em from down in that cellar a'yours?"

"Shut up, Ward."

Smiling, Ward leaned back in his chair and pulled his hat low, down over his eyes. "Night, Matt."

Jason was surprised to find Saul awake and outside as he made his rounds. Saul seemed just as startled as Jason. In fact, he leaped to his feet and braced himself, fists up, before he relaxed and said, "Oh. Hello, Jason."

Jason grinned and motioned at Saul to sit back down. "What the heck are you doing up and awake, Saul?"

"The crate in the storeroom isn't very conducive to slumber, I'm afraid," he said, settling back on the stoop.

"Wouldn't Rachael—"

"Her cot's too narrow, and she's still hurting," Saul explained.

"Sorry." Jason sat down next to him.

"Thanks."

"Saul?"

"What's preying on your mind, Jason?"

Jason tipped his head. "What makes you ask that?"

"Something is, isn't it? You're up walking the streets at three in the morning, aren't you?"

Saul had him there. He said, "I'm just nervous about tomorrow, I guess. I wish somebody around here had a big-time mining operation going."

Saul hiked his eyebrows.

"For a supply of dynamite, you know?"

Saul nodded sagely, then asked, "You're wanting to burn them, then blow them up, too? Would you not call that overkill?"

Jason grinned. "I reckon you're right, Saul. I just wish I was more sure of that thing with the oil."

"And kerosene."

"Right. And kerosene."

"It will work, Jason. My Rachael says so, and she is hardly ever wrong in matters of importance."

Jason nodded. "Hardly ever wrong." Then slowly, he shook his head. "Makes me feel a whole lot better, Saul." He stood up. "Thanks."

Saul got up from the stoop, too. "I didn't mean to make you feel that way, Jason. I was just saying that Rachael explained to me what you were doing, and why it would work. She remembered how I accidentally set her father's shed on fire, just after we were wed. There was a place out behind the shed where her mother used to toss the used-up cooking oil, and—"

"Right. I've got my rounds to finish, Saul."

Saul wrinkled his brow again. "I'm sorry if I—"

Calling, "See you later," over his shoulder, Jason stalked off down the street toward the south gate, leaving Saul with nothing but silence.

Jason made a hard left at the gate, walked past the Milchers' church, and proceeded down to the stable, where he stuck his head in long enough to determine that everybody in the makeshift hospital was asleep. As he moved on down the boardwalk, he began to regret his attitude toward Saul. He shouldn't have spoken—or not spoken—to Saul that way.

It was he who was the problem, not Saul. And it was he who was acting like a six-year-old.

Without thinking, he slugged the front wall of

Copeland's Millinery and immediately regretted it. And was angry at Copeland for not painting his wife's hat and ribbon shop earlier, because he ended up with splinters in his knuckles.

Cursing under his breath, he tugged at the splinters with teeth and fingernails, and still didn't have all of them out by the time he rounded the square and ended up back at the jail again. The light was on, and he walked in to find Matt MacDonald asleep in his cell and Ward Wanamaker dozing at the desk, his head pillowed on an open seed catalogue.

He walked over to the desk, moved Ward's elbow enough to open the side drawer and pull out the tweezers—all without waking Ward—then sat down in the opposite chair and pulled the lamp closer. His nose inches from his sore knuckles—which in the light looked like the spine of a ratty porcupine—he began pulling splinters.

"That's quite a mess you got there," Ward said, and Jason jumped, stabbing himself with the tweezers in the process.

"Ouch!" he snarled, and looked up. "Let a man know you're awake, why don't you?"

"Sorry, didn't know you was so interested," Ward said. He pointed to Jason's bad hand. "Aimin' at somebody in particular?"

"Myself. I missed."

"You don't say." Ward twisted his head. "Musta been some kind of a piece of lumber that got in your way."

Carefully, Jason pulled out a new splinter before he said, "Yup. Was attached to the millinery."

Thoughtfully, Ward sniffed. "Worst kind. I hear they're vicious."

Jason nodded and attached his tweezers to a new splinter. It was the last one he could see extending from the skin, although he could surely feel more of them in there.

Ward suddenly lifted his head. "You hear that?"

"Hear what?

"Hush up. Listen."

Jason held his tongue, but he still didn't hear anything out of place. "You're getting daffy, Ward. What time is it anyway?" He could just make out the first streaks of red and orange on the western horizon. It made him feel itchy inside.

Ward looked past Jason's shoulder to the clock on the wall. "Quarter past five."

Jason's internal alarm went off. At any minute they could be swarming with Apache! He shot to his feet so quickly that he knocked his chair over backward and said, "Wake up Matt and send him over to the stables. With a rifle. You stay put, gimp. If they make it over the wall, shoot yourself."

"Shoot myself?"

"You do it, it'll be fast. They do it for you, it'll take days." He jerked open the door. "You pick."

He went to Saul's place first. Saul had dozed off on the stoop, his back against a support and his feet propped on an upturned bucket.

Jason walked up beside him and shoved his shoulder,

knocking him over sideways, but catching him before he could tip all the way over. "Sorry, Saul. Wake up." Saul's eyes were barely halfway open as Jason dragged him up to his feet. "C'mon, Saul, up and at 'em!"

"What?"

"I said, get up. It's practically dawn and the Philistines are coming."

"What?"

He heard a distant rustle, like far-off buckskin rubbing low brush, and he gave Saul another shake. "I'm sorry for how I was before," he said, hoping it made some sense. "But it's morning, and the Apache are about to attack. Or might be about to. Understand?"

Saul nodded and pulled free of Jason's grip. "Dawn. Apache. Right," Saul said, coming swiftly to his full senses. "I'll wake the others."

"You take the south and east sides, I'll take the north and the west."

"Indeed," Saul said, and jogged away to the south, sluggishly tripping as he went. The last Jason heard of him, he was beating on the door of Rollie Biggston's place and calling for Abigail to get up and get moving.

9

"Did you hear what he said?" asked Treat Paris. Beneath his shaggy brown hair, his boyish face was scrunched up like a perplexed monkey's.

"What? What who said?" Jesse Fig, the freight wagon's other driver, looked up from the piece of leather he was mending.

"That kid sheriff they got," Treat went on, exasperated with Jesse. Nothing was worse than a one-eyed mule skinner, unless it was a one-eyed mule skinner from Tennessee. Which Jesse was.

"Sheriff was just here," Treat went on, keeping his voice loud and clear, as if Jesse's missing eye somehow affected his ears, too. "Did you hear what he said? Any of it?"

"Huh?" Jesse drawled, finally looking up from the leather. "Who was here?"

"Cripes, Jesse, you beat everything, you know that?" Treat shouted, and stalked off to the stable.

Behind him, he heard Jesse say, "Treat? Treat, what you talkin' 'bout? Treat?"

But Treat just kept on walking. His Winchester was snug in his hand as he climbed one of the ladders behind the stable and came to rest on the wide plank affixed to the stockade wall. A series of them circled the wall as far as he could see, and every ten feet or so was a man with a rifle or a handgun, with more men on the way.

"Morning," said a lanky fellow crouched down the way, to his right. The mayor, if Treat remembered correctly.

"Morning, Mayor," he replied as he moved closer. The man sure looked like a mayor anyway. He wore a light gray suit, all matched up, unlike the rest of them. They were a ratty-looking bunch, all right, and he was the first to admit it.

"It's just Salmon," said the mayor. "You're Treat, right? From the wagon train?"

"That's me," Treat answered. Salmon? What were his folks thinking, naming him after a fish?

Slowly, Treat shook the mayor named after a fish out of his mind and raised his head, taking a long look out over the land to the south. There was nothing. Nothing at all. No dust trails, no signs of movement, no little patches of color out of place. Nothing even slightly unusual.

Or so he assumed.

"What did we pay you for the oil and kerosene, Treat?" Salmon asked.

Treat shrugged his shoulders. "Don't know. Ask our wagon master."

"I will."

"Anybody check the fording place lately, Salmon?" he asked as, out of nothing but habit, he checked his gun.

"No, everybody's been a little busy, in case you weren't paying attention," the mayor said curtly.

"Sorry. Just wondering when we might be able to pull out."

"You'll have to ask Jason about that," Kendall said, annoyance seeping into his voice. "The sheriff, that is. I imagine he'll want you fellows to stick close for a while. For your own good naturally."

"Naturally," Treat repeated. It would just figure, wouldn't it? They'd have this backwoods boy sheriff holding them here forever. Didn't he realize they had a schedule to meet?

Probably not. Treat doubted anybody who lived this far out in the middle of nowhere realized much of anything besides dinnertime. And he had his doubts about that.

"Hey, Treat." With some surprise, he realized it was Jesse.

"Decide to join us?" he asked, somewhat sarcastically.

It was lost on Jesse. He said, "You fellers see anythin' out there, Injun-wise?"

Treat opened his mouth to say, "Nothing," but the word didn't have time to come out. Before he could speak, a cacophony of war cries split the morning stillness, shocking at least two men further down the line clean off the planks they'd been standing on.

Out of reflex, Treat stood, nestled the barrel of his rifle between the spiky tops of the stockade posts, and got off a shot. Which hit absolutely nothing.

Angry with himself, he cocked the rifle again and

this time took more careful aim. He'd have to wait. They were too far out, but they were charging like there was no tomorrow. And it seemed there were twice as many of them as before.

Couldn't be, he thought, perplexed. *You're letting this thing get to you. Buck up.*

"Light your wicks!" Salmon yelled down the line, then turned the other way and yelled it again.

For a minute, Treat thought the mayor had gone peach-orchard crazy until Salmon looked right at Treat and said, "Wake up, man! Light that wick!"

Then Treat remembered the wicks they'd run from the kegs yesterday, and he reached toward his pocket for a lucifer while he searched the tops of the posts. The wicks were spaced out about every twenty feet or so, he recalled.

Amazingly, Jesse found it before he did, and pointed it out. Treat moved about five feet to the east, grabbed the wick before Jesse had a chance to, and flicked his lucifer into life.

Once he was certain the wick was burning, he let it drop to the ground outside, twenty feet below. If he'd been a genuflecting sort of man, he would have crossed himself.

As it was, he just said a silent prayer that it wouldn't go out until it ignited that keg of kerosene—and all that whale oil they'd poured out into the ditch.

On the north wall, Jason heard Kendall's order to light the kegs, and repeated it as Salmon had, to his right and to his left. He figured that the Apache would likely come around to the north side pretty quickly once they saw the fire and smoke coming from the ditch on the south.

That is, if the ditch caught.

If the kerosene worked.

If there was still enough oil in the ditch—oil close enough to the surface anyhow—to burn for a while.

If he hadn't gone stark raving loony.

If, if, if.

The first keg that caught was on the southeast corner, and only because one of the boys tired of the fuse burning for so long and just shot it. It went up in a whoosh and spread quickly down the ditch, feeding on the whale oil, which had remained very present over the past twenty-four hours, and imploding keg after keg of kerosene.

The explosions surprised not only the men on the wall, but three or four braves who had made it down into the ditch—and were abruptly blown high in the air and out of sight.

Soon, every man jack of them was shooting at the barrels as it if were a carnival game, and just as quickly, the perimeter was encircled by a moat of smoke and flame.

The men in the town couldn't see the Indians anymore, but they hadn't gone away. As Jason had suspected, the war chief sent half his men around the town to the north, and they quickly had Fury basically surrounded.

As instructed, the Apache backed off far enough to stay clear of shots from the walls, and settled in to wait.

Even the Apache knew that a fire could not burn forever.

Not even one so big as the white men had made for their town.

Inside, the inhabitants were starting a premature celebration. That is, until Jason put a stop to it.

But the damage had been done. Women were already starting to venture timidly out into the streets, more than half the men who had been on the south wall were down on the ground, and a bandaged and heavily medicated Rollie Biggston had declared free drinks for the next hour.

Jason moved through the crowds, trying to get men back up on the wall, trying to get the women inside, but he enjoyed little success.

"They're gone, Jason!" said one of the citizens, who had already taken obvious advantage of Biggston's largesse. "Quit bein' such a worrywart!"

Jason shoved him rudely to the ground and stalked off.

What did these people have, a death wish? He knew those Apache were still out there, waiting for the fire to die down, waiting for a break in the line, waiting for the chance to get just a few men inside and murder them all.

If there was one thing an Apache could do, it was wait.

He didn't want his sister killed by the Apache. He didn't much like the idea for Megan either. And when he'd told Ward to shoot himself, he hadn't been kidding.

The Indians must be plenty ticked off by now, and if they got hold of any of his people, they were liable to work out their frustration on them in the worst possible way anybody could imagine.

He saw a few lonely figures still on the south wall, and picked out Saul's form up on the planks, his back against the stockade wall. Jason broke into a trot and hurried over.

"Now what?" was the first thing that Saul said to him when he climbed up the ladder.

Jason shrugged. "I seem to have lost control of the situation. So don't ask me."

"You didn't think they would just see our fires and go home?"

"No way."

Saul nodded. "Then I was right to stay here when the others left. Even our Mayor Kendall has made a trip to Biggston's." He shook his head disapprovingly.

Jason wasn't surprised. It seemed like half the town— and all of the wagon drivers—were inside Biggston's or outside, drinking in the street.

He just hoped that they could shoot when they were drunk. And that they could actually hit their bobbing and weaving targets.

Hell, half of them couldn't hit a bull's-eye target when they were ten feet away and sober as judges. And that was on a good day.

Jason sank to his heels and rested his brow on his knees.

"If you are praying, I hope your God is listening to you today," he heard Saul say.

Jason slowly looked up. "I hope so, too. Hope

somebody's God is. But we're going to need more than divine intervention."

Saul looked shocked, and Jason chuckled.

"What?" said Saul, incredulous at this heresy. "More than God you think you're needing?"

"Just afraid I'm gonna have to get Him a little help, Saul."

"Help?"

"Trust me," Jason said, and climbed back down the ladder.

"Don't take offense, Jason, but I'd rather put my faith in the Lord," Saul shouted after him.

Thinking that he'd rather do that, too, if only the situation permitted it, Jason hurried across the street. But he didn't stop at the jail. He headed west until he came to the first house off the square—which was his house.

"Jenny?" he called, walking in the front door. "Jen? Megan? You here?"

Jenny stuck her blond head out of the kitchen, followed by Megan's russet mop. "What is it?" they said as one.

"I want to talk to both of you," he said as he plucked his hat from his head. He strode into the kitchen and sat down at the table. "Sit," he commanded.

Like puppies, they plopped down into two facing chairs.

"What is it?" Jenny asked again.

At least they hadn't gone outside to check on the sounds of celebration and been swept up in the town's foolishness. But he was going to ask them to do something far less dim-witted and far more daring.

And far more dangerous.

Forearms propped on the table, he leaned toward them. "Girls," he began, "do you remember when we were comin' out here?"

Jenny and Megan looked at each other as if silently confirming that he was crazy.

And maybe he was.

But he went on anyway, went on in a rush, barely stopping for air. And the girls listened, openmouthed.

But they listened.

10

The wagon train

Bound and determined to make up the day they'd lost, Blake and the others ate while they rode or drove.

Blake himself was riding his horse, Buck, today, and keeping his cup of coffee balanced on the wagon seat, beside his wife, Laura, and their infant son.

Laura drove a team as well as any man, and he had no worries about her. Other than the fact that she was always so enthralled with the beauty of the mornings out here— the colors in the dawn sky, the soft butter yellow and lavenders and blues and pinks of the vast stretches of wildflowers in the distance—she managed to stay on track. Becky Mankiller was just as adept, but Olin Whaler's wife, Lena, was a tad shaky as a teamster.

It didn't help that her boys were more intent on horsing around than on giving her any assistance. And her husband was riding far out to their right side, paying no mind to anybody or anything.

Randy Mankiller rode up beside Blake. He nodded

hello, then said, "You wanna kill them Whaler boys yourself, or can I?"

"Oh, you don't need to go that far, Randy," Blake said.

"Oh, all right. I'll just take out Olin then."

Blake reached out and grabbed Randy's reins before he could head out toward Olin. "Easy does it there, buddy."

Bemused, Randy shook his head. "You're takin' all the fun outta this for me, Blake."

"Sorry to be such a joy killer."

The two rode in silence for a bit. Then Randy said, "When you figure we'll hit Fury?"

"Maybe a couple of days, if we can avoid attracting any Apache's attention. Maybe longer."

"You don't got any idea where we are, do you?"

"Not a clue. I'm just trying to follow what trail the Express rider left."

"That's not much," said Randy, looking around.

"Tell me about it. When we get closer, though, we'll cut to the old Mormon Trail. That'll be easier to follow."

"What with the broken glass and jugs and all?"

"Check." Actually, he was searching for the Mormon Trail right now. He was weary of traveling blind, and wanted some nice shiny broken glass—or even some old worn trail ruts—to follow.

"Hey, Rev!"

Both Randy and Blake looked over toward Olin, who was broadly waving at them although he was still scowling.

He yelled again. "I found the Trail! Over this way!"

Randy looked back at Blake. "You reckon we should take a look?" he asked dryly.

Blake shrugged, although he was thrilled with Olin's news. "Might's well."

The two set off at a lope toward Olin, and the four wagons slowly, joltingly followed them.

Lone Wolf's growling stomach told him it was time for the midday meal, but he was fixated on the curtain of smoke still rising from the ditch around the town. One of his men, Works Like Beaver, rode up from down the line. He had been one of the braves to ride north, and Lone Wolf looked toward him anxiously.

Works Like Beaver slid from his pony and approached, bowing his head in acknowledgment to his war chief. Lone Wolf returned the gesture, and held his hand out to indicate that Works Like Beaver might be seated on the blanket across the small cook fire from him.

When the newcomer was seated and comfortable, Lone Wolf asked him, "What news do you carry?"

"The condition is the same there as here. Much smoke and fire, so that a man may not see past it, nor find a path through it. And it is the same in all directions, Lone Wolf."

Lone Wolf grunted. "And what is it they burn which lasts for so long?" He had asked the question more of himself than anyone else, but Works Like Beaver answered it.

"It is not wood or dried cactus or dung. It is as if they

have figured a way to make the earth itself sprout fire."
Works Like Beaver lowered his eyes to the ground. "It
is like magic." He raised his eyes again. "Do you think
it possible that their god has intervened for them? Do
you think that—"

"No," Lone Wolf replied, cutting him off. "It is not
possible. Their god is no god at all. How can he be?
How can a single god control everything: wind, fire,
sorrow, happiness, rain, the animals, and on and on?
Not possible."

Works Like Beaver grunted in agreement. Lone Wolf
was right. It was not possible that everything known by
man—and everything yet to be learned—was controlled
by a single god. He said, "Then what? What have they
done to make the earth burn as if it were made of coal?"

Lone Wolf pondered this for a time. Then he asked,
"They did not fill the ditch with coal, did they?"

Works Like Beaver shook his head. "It is the earth
itself that burns. They dug down to the place where the
ground is hard and soft all at once, and set it on fire. It
burns long and steady, as we have all seen."

Lone Wolf shook his head. This layer of ground had
been long known to his people. They, and their neigh-
bors the Navajo as well as other tribes in the area, used
it to make pots. It did not catch flame and smoke when
they fired it in their kilns.

It did not catch fire at all.

How could it burn now? What reason could there be
for it to catch fire and hold it for so long?

He did not know. At least, he could not think of an
immediate answer.

His stomach growled again and he slapped at it. "You can leave," he said to Works Like Beaver. "I will send for you if need be." He waved toward the main cook fire. "Get yourself sustenance."

And when Works Like Beaver asked him if he might bring him food, too, he said, "No, I have pemmican," and shook a little leather bag at his side, as if to prove his point.

In truth, he was not eating.

He was waiting for a sign, some kind of mystical glamour, to show him the how and why of the smoke and fire before he would allow food to touch his lips. He had already sent three braves to the creek to haul water to put it out—to no avail.

They said they hauled much water, and it had no effect. It sank into the hot, thirsty soil beside the clay, and that was all. It neither increased nor decreased the amount of flame, but slightly intensified the smoke rising from it.

And Gray Fox, the only man who had survived the explosion in the trench this morning, was burned beyond recognition and singing his death song beneath a canopied wolf's hide at the far south of their ranks.

It was a great puzzlement.

Curly and the other hands had spent the night down in the bunkhouse hidey-hole after a long day with no boss around. They rose carefully with the dawn, and seeing no sign of Indians, had made coffee and bacon and toast for their breakfasts. It wasn't much compared to their usual fare, but they figured it was better to travel on light stomachs for now.

They'd been right.

At half past six, Curly spotted thick gray smoke rising to the north. Town. He couldn't be certain what the source was—the Indians or the townspeople—but he figured it wouldn't do him any good to look on the sunny side of things.

He rounded up the boys—easy, for they were huddled in a corner of the bunkhouse—and everybody took to the cellar again. Curly told the boys that if they had to spend much more time down here, he was applying for miner's wages.

The laughter was minimal.

They sat down there for what seemed like hours—and was—before they heard the Indians hit them. At first, it was distant and far away, as if they were ransacking the main house first.

Makes sense, Curly thought, his lips twisting into a scowl. Mr. and Mrs. MacDonald had a lot of nice things, things they got from the occasional freighters that came through Fury. And Mr. MacDonald had a lot of money to spend.

He heard distant whoops of laughter, and the far-off ripping, tinkling sound of wood breaking and glass smashing. The latter was most probably pretty Mrs. MacDonald's curio cabinet with all its glass shelves and little figurines. Mostly horses, they were.

What a shame, he thought with a slow shake of his head. Some of those little figures were downright cunning.

* * *

Having left the girls back at the house scurrying for rifles and ammunition, Jason made his way down to Rollie Biggston's place, where he walked in the back door and took Abigail aside.

"From now on," he said, "you tell every man you serve that it's his last, and as soon as he finishes up, he's to report to his station on the wall. You got me?"

"Y-yes, Jason," she said, eyes wide. "Why? Isn't the trouble over with?"

"No, it's not, Abby," he said. "And after the last man's been served his last drink, you get yourself someplace safe. Unless . . . how are you with a rifle?"

"Me? I'd hardly know which end to point!"

"Then get yourself someplace safe, for sure."

As he turned, she caught his sleeve. "Down in the cellar, where Rollie keeps the good stuff?"

"Yeah, and take Rollie down there with you. He's not ready to climb up the wall yet, and the hospital's pretty full up."

Her fingers released his sleeve. "All right, Jason. And about the wall? Between you and me, Rollie can't climb it even when he's Sunday-go-to-meetin' sober."

For the briefest of instants, Jason smiled. "Good girl."

As he turned away again and walked out through the crowd, she smiled at him admiringly.

Once Jason got clear of the crowd, he looked up the street to see Megan and Jenny headed his way, each loaded down with a rifle and a small leather pouch of ammunition. He waved to get their attention, and met them in the middle of the street.

"We're ready," announced Jenny, all business. "Where do you want us?"

"For the moment, I want you rounding up the other women who know which end of a rifle to point," he said.

"All right," said Megan, nodding. "I know just where to start."

"And once we finish that?"

"Then I want you up on the wall," Jason said. "Fight like you would for our father, Jenny."

She didn't look the slightest bit intimidated. "I will, Jason."

"Me, too," Megan echoed.

"And if you see your husband," Jason went on, still looking toward Jenny, "don't shoot him. Save the bullet for a deserving Apache."

"You take all the fun out of things, Jason."

"I know."

Rifle balanced over his shoulder, he walked off down toward the jail.

This time, Ward was awake when Jason walked in. But he still had Matt MacDonald in a cell. Matt was sleeping like a baby.

"What's with him?" Jason asked, pointing. "Thought you were going to send him up on the wall."

"Had him up and almost out a while back. Little turd

kept tryin' to leave town, even after they lit the fires."
Ward poured himself a cup of coffee and one for Jason.
"Finally ended up crackin' him over the head and drag-
gin' him back down here. The son of a gun's been out
ever since."

Jason took a sip of his coffee. "This is good stuff," he
said. Generally speaking, it left Ward's usual brew in the
dust, and he took another drink just to make sure that
his taste buds weren't playing a trick on him.

They weren't.

"I didn't make it," Ward said as if he were reading
Jason's mind. "Mrs. Morelli come by and brewed it up."

"Thank you, Olympia," Jason said to the air.

Ward nodded his agreement. He tipped his head
toward Matt. "What you want me to do with him? Personally, I'm in favor of lettin' him out the gate, except
we might have to let four or five Apaches in to make it
a fair trade."

Jason nodded and pulled out a chair. He sat down.
"Agreed. Let's just keep him where he is for the mean-
time, all right? If he wakes and starts getting uppity
again, get some of that sleeping powder from Doc
Morelli and sneak it into his coffee. Doc won't mind so
long as you tell him it's for good ol' Matthew."

Ward took another sip of coffee. "You're the sheriff."

"Unfortunately."

Ward hiked a brow. "Why? What's goin' on out
there?"

"You name it. My list got too long to remember."

"The Apache ain't gone then?"

Jason gave his head a slow shake. "I don't think so,

but I can't see a dang thing through the smoke. What I think is that they're still out there, waiting for the fire to burn itself out. Which it will, sooner or later."

Ward's brows went up one at a time. "You could be right, y'know, Jason." He nodded, and began to precariously rock back and forth on the straight legs of his chair. "Yessir, you sure could."

Jason didn't answer him. Instead, he poured himself a second cup of coffee. If he was going to die, it might as well be with the taste of good, fresh coffee on his lips.

After he took the first hot, clean gulp into his mouth and savored it, he swallowed and asked, "Ward, are you a godly man?"

"You mean, do I go to church of a Sunday? At the Milchers'?"

Jason didn't go to Milcher's church either, so he said, "No, I mean, do you believe in God?"

"Sure do," Ward said. "My mama would've tanned my hide iff'n I wasn't. Or didn't, I mean." Ward looked confused. "Wasn't?"

"Then start praying now," Jason said, ignoring Ward's fuddle and throwing back the last of his coffee as he climbed to his feet. "Make sure you pray for the right side." He set his empty cup back on the stove. "And stay in this jail. I don't want you trying to climb the wall yet. And again, if the Apache break through the wall and get in here, shoot yourself."

Ward's brows flew up.

"I mean it. Don't let them get at you."

Ward swallowed hard, but he said, "Right. You can count on me."

Jason nodded and walked out, closing the door behind him.

Outside on the street, he saw a large knot of grumbling men near the circled trade wagons, and he moved toward it. "Howdy, men," he called once he was within hailing distance.

One of the men turned around. "You know who stopped the liquor, buddy?"

Jason kept a friendly smile on his face. "I did, friend. I'm afraid we're gonna have a few more Indians to fight today."

"What makes you think that?" the man snarled. "Nobody's heard a peep outta them since the fires was lit."

"Can you see them through the smoke?" Jason asked.

"Hell, no. They all run away."

"Just because you can't see 'em, that doesn't mean they aren't out there," Jason said genially. "We don't intend to take any chances."

The man's hand dropped toward his gun. "And just who the hell are you to say what the town is or isn't gonna do?"

Still smiling, Jason's right hand dropped to within reach of his gun while his left thumbed aside his jacket lapel to reveal his badge.

"I'm Jason Fury. The town sheriff. Any more questions, gents?"

He was vastly relived when the men grumbled *no,* and turned to head back to the stockade walls.

11

Down at the MacDonald place, Curly, hiding beneath the bunkhouse floor with the two other hands, heard the fall of soft footsteps on the floorboards above. The three of them froze at the first rustle, and Curly held his fingers to his lips before he silently blew out the lantern.

They waited, sweat pouring from their every pore, each moccasin footfall sounding to them like the beat of a big bass drum. At one point, one of those footsteps landed on the timber directly above Carlos's head, and Curly had to practically strangle him to keep him from crying out.

They listened while the braves threw their bedding around, opened and slammed shut drawers and doors, and even pulled the potbellied stove from the floor. Or at least, did something that sounded like it.

Curly was mad, about as angry as he'd ever been in his life, but he tamped it back and held his tongue. He knew there was enough kerosene up there that if the Apache learned where they were hiding, they'd only have to crack open the hatch to pour enough flaming fuel through the crack to roast them alive.

He wasn't going to die that way. All he could do was wait them out and pray that he and the hands wouldn't be discovered. They were lower down than the braves above, and it would be a miracle if they made it up top with their heads still on their shoulders.

At long last, it seemed his prayers for deliverance were answered. After one last kick to the stove—or at least what sounded like a kick to the stove—the braves withdrew.

Muffled footsteps exited the bunkhouse, and a little while later, they heard the distant sound of hoofbeats as the savages left.

"Wait," Curly whispered when one man reached for the latch. "Give them a few minutes." Just because they'd gone away, it didn't mean they'd gone far.

The hand retreated, and Curly waited. After five minutes had passed, he felt the boards above him. He was searching for heat, but there was none. Softly, he said, "Listen, fellas, Apache usually burn everything they run across, and—"

"*Sí,*" said Carlos. "They burn my whole village when I was a boy, only seven. They are murderous pigs," he added, then spat.

"Whoa," whispered Wilmer, whose bony hand had just grabbed for the latch and rested there, trembling. "Your mama, she make it?"

"My *mamacita* made me hide down the well," Carlos continued, without answering the question directly.

"Quiet!" hissed Wilmer.

"And you, too, Wilmer," whispered Curly. "They might have left somebody up there to catch us."

"So now we wait longer?" Carlos murmured.

"Yep," said Curly. "Give it just five more minutes, okay?"

"*Sí,*" said Carlos.

"Yeah," agreed a shaken Wilmer.

Curly relaxed a little. He'd only made out four separate voices among the Apache, so they hadn't sent the whole mob. Probably just a scouting party who had found no one at the ranch, and probably assumed everybody was in town. Burning.

His stomach roiled at the thought. He didn't care so much about Mr. MacDonald as he did about Miss Megan and Mrs. MacDonald. But it was a terrible fate for anybody, to burn up. Especially to burn at an Apache's hand. He had seen it once, when he was young and a trooper. It was why he was so cautious now.

At last, he figured the five minutes were up and it was time to face whatever was—or was not—out there. He said, "Okay, Wilmer. Open it just a crack."

Slowly, Wilmer pushed aside the crossbeam and opened up the trapdoor about half an inch.

"A little more," whispered Curly.

Wilmer pushed it up another half inch. Enough that Curly could see the tipped-over stove, could see and smell its ashes, and smell the spilt kerosene. He could also hear the faint whoops of four Apache, who, by the sound of things, had set the main house on fire.

"Close 'er up, Wilmer," he said to the older man. Those hoofbeats he'd heard must have come from their own horses, which they'd left up in the paddock. "We're gonna be down here for a while longer."

Wilmer, who had seen and heard exactly what Curly had, was more than happy to comply.

Outside, four braves watched the main house burning, watched the walls slowly go up in flame, and cheered when part of the roof fell in and down to the ground, bringing part of the second floor and a slide of furniture with it. Shy Colt went so far as to jump in the horse trough with delight.

But Cunning Dog wasn't so overjoyed. There were many more things to burn, here: a barn, a pump shed, a sleeping house. He pulled Shy Colt from the water and sent him, along with Sees Far, to learn if there was any livestock in the barn. If they could find no whites to kill, perhaps they might find cattle or horses to steal.

Tipping Hawk he sent to set fire to the shed, while he went to take a torch from the house with which to set the workers' sleeping house ablaze.

Shy Colt and Sees Far came back with a milk cow, a calf—perhaps a week old—at her heels, and two ducks who immediately headed for the water trough Shy Colt had vacated earlier, flew up, and began to swim in it.

Cunning Dog asked, "This was all?"

Both braves nodded.

"Kill the calf. We will eat." Cunning Dog, having spoken, turned toward the shed. Tipping Hawk had set it aflame—something the other two had neglected to do to the barn.

But Shy Colt was now busy butchering the calf while Sees Far strained to hold back its bawling, frantic mother.

Idiots.

Still holding his torch, Cunning Dog started toward the sleeping house, and started round it, setting flame to every protruding board he could find. By the time he had rounded it, the whole building, dry as the desert trees from which it had been built, was blazing, and the roof had caught.

By that time, Tipping Hawk had jogged back up to the barn and set fire to that.

Cunning Dog grunted with satisfaction. They had done their job, and done it well. And they would have livestock to take. They had found three horses, plus the cow, plus the ducks.

Having tethered the cow to a fence post, Sees Far was now helping Shy Dog peel the hide from the calf's carcass and then push a spit through the animal's body. Together, they carried it to the edge of the burning house and hoisted it onto the Y-shaped posts they had already set into the ground on either side of the impromptu roasting fire. Within minutes, the fine smell of cooking flesh came to his nostrils.

They had burned many buildings and taken some animals.

Life was good. And Lone Wolf would be pleased.

The people in the town could not see it, for it was veiled by the still-rising smoke from their ditch, but the smoke rising from the south was obvious to Lone Wolf and those Apaches on the south side of the town. A few cheered, but were quickly quieted. They had at least done some damage today.

Lone Wolf hoped that besides Fiery Hair, there had been many white settlers at the ranch that his men had burned. He hoped they had all been tortured, and had died in agony. Screaming. Even the women and children. He hoped the babies had been thrown against the walls of the houses or fences made of spikes, that their skulls had split open, and that their mothers had been made to watch as they died.

He had far worse things planned for the townspeople, but it would be a good start.

The smoke was just beginning to thin its cloak around the town. Perhaps this white trick would fade in time. He could wait.

He had time.

By four o'clock the Apaches had gone and Curly, Carlos, and Wilmer had nearly suffocated in the small cellar beneath the bunkhouse. But they struggled out, fighting their way through the flames that still rose from all around them, fighting past the heavy roof beam that had toppled across the trapdoor.

No more roof, no more bunks.

And when, coughing and hacking, they made their way out into the yard, the house was nothing more than a pile of smoldering, smoking timber. The barn and shed were gone, too, and Wilmer made his way up to what was left of the barn first thing.

Probably to check on the cow and her calf, Curly thought. He also thought it likely that they were both dead, buried in the rubble, although he said nothing. He couldn't speak anyway. He tried, and was surprised when no sound came out, only a feeble puff of thin smoke.

Wilmer came back down to where the house had been and spread his hands, shrugging his shoulders. Apparently there was no cow to be found. But Carlos had found something. He waved them over to the front corner of the rubble pile.

They found the calf's remains—little more than a few bones still clinging to a rough spit—and a few feet away, Carlos found the little thing's guts and hide.

Poor Missus, Curly thought, thinking of Jenny. That calf had been her and Miss Megan's pet. Trouble, they called him, because his mama had had such a hard time bringing him into the world.

Judging by the tracks, the Apache had ridden their horses off and led the cow. At least, there were shod prints mingled with the unshod prints made by their ponies. He hoped that his horse, Spin, took it into his head to buck that brave—or braves, if they were riding double—clear back to Texas.

And right smack on top of a cactus.

Drat them anyway!

"Jenny!" Jason called.

From atop the platform affixed to the interior of the stockade, Jenny turned around and shouted, "What?"

She looked irritated, Jason thought, but then he'd be, too, if he were her. She was obviously still upset with her marital situation, and had run away from it—something against her nature to begin with—to find herself thrust into the role of a soldier, rifle and all, defending the town's perimeter.

She should be back East somewhere, attending Miss So-and-So's Academy of China Painting or some such, Jason thought. Not on the run from both a husband and a force of Apache warriors.

But then, his sister was a force of nature, wasn't she?

"What is it, Jason?" she repeated.

He waved her over and, bless her heart, she came. Not happily, but she did. He started toward her, and they met on the south side of the square. He spoke first. "Can you do me another favor, Jenny?"

She didn't say yes or no, just stared at him. But she didn't walk away, so he figured he was still in her good graces. He said, "Jenny, I want you to round up the womenfolk and have them get their old kitchen grease and household oil."

She still didn't say a thing, but she was looking at him as if he'd just lost his mind.

"I want them to take it up on the wall and toss it over, into the moat. You understand? And the more they can scrape up, the better."

"Any kind?"

"Anything," he said, nodding. "Beef fat, bacon grease, chicken fat, cooking oil, shortening, anything. Just collect it in wooden buckets, and when they're full, chuck 'em down into the moat."

She turned on her heel and left to go about her mission, calling over her shoulder, "By the way, my house is on fire."

"Jenny?" he called after her, but she was too far away to hear.

Then he talked to some of the men from the freight wagons and also most of the townsmen, asking them to gather everything slightly combustible that they might have—axle grease, liniment, hair oil, hinge oil, and the like—and sent them on their way to make collections.

Soon, the smoke changed from dark gray to black as buckets filled with everything from chicken grease to pig fat to horse liniment to hair oil were tossed over the fence and into the ditch.

"That should hold them for the night," he muttered as he watched fresh billows of smoke rise above the stockade. "And maybe into the morning, too."

"What the hell you burnin' now?" said Ward's voice from behind him.

"Dinner grease," replied Jason. "What are you doing out of the office?"

Ward patted his pocket. "Had to see the doc about our boarder. I picked up a little surprise for Matt."

Jason grinned. "Well, aren't you just a daisy?"

Ward chuckled. "Oh, that's just how I think'a myself. A regular flower."

They started toward the jailhouse.

The wagon train

"You sure you don't see anything?" asked Mankiller, looking west, his hand shading his eyes.

The Reverend Blake shook his head. "No, nothing. But then, I'm a little nearsighted." He, too, squinted at the far western horizon.

Both men were on horseback, and both had ridden down the Mormon Trail far ahead of the wagons. Mankiller was standing in his stirrups. He wasn't the nearsighted one, and he was certain that he'd seen a puff of smoke on the far horizon.

Well, maybe it had been a cloud. Or a mirage.

But it had been something, something that moved a bit, then faded away.

The faint jingle of harness came to his ears. He said, "That'll be the wagons comin' up."

The Reverend Blake nodded curtly. "We'll drop back and keep pace with them. And don't mention this to anybody, Randy. Okay? Just keep those sharp eyes of yours peeled."

Mankiller understood. The reverend didn't want to cause any confusion in the ranks. Meaning Olin Whaler specifically.

"Right," Randy said, reining his horse around. "I can keep my trap shut."

Blake, too, turned his mount back toward the east alongside Randy Mankiller's. They began to jog back toward the nearing wagons.

"You're a good man, Randy."

"Try my best."

"You succeed. Now, if I could only get you to be a God-fearing man . . ."

Randy grinned. "Fat chance, Rev. My daddy reared

me on all the gods of the Cherokee, and let me tell you, they're a colorful bunch. Yours don't stand a chance."

"We'll see about that," said Blake, grinning a tad, and kicked his horse into a canter.

Randy kept pace.

12

It didn't work out quite the way Jason had planned.

The fires began to peter out at about four in the morning, and the men still up on the stockade were forced to start shooting at around four forty-five, with the very first feeble rays of morning light.

It started on the north side, and within ten minutes of firing the first round, the townsmen had killed or wounded sixteen braves. The Apache, however, had wounded seven settlers and killed one.

The south side wasn't faring much better.

Jason took no comfort in that, though. He was busy running from house to house, rousting out possible shooters who were still asleep and making certain that the wounded made it to the livery.

Doc Morelli was already busy tending the wounded. Even his wife was going from cot to cot, passing out coffee or water and slabs of toasted bread with melted cheese to the maimed and injured who felt well enough to eat.

Jenny and Megan were already up on the wall, and had been responsible for putting three braves out of commission between them. When Jason climbed up to see how they were doing, Jenny told him that they were just fine, thank you very much, and to go help somebody who needed it.

As he was climbing back down the ladder, he heard Jenny's whoop of "Four!"

They were holding their own, he guessed, but for how much longer? There were hundreds of determined and bloodthirsty savages out there who would just as soon slice them from stem to stern as, well, slice them from stern to stem. As it were.

He shook his head to try to rattle the sense back into it.

And then he jumped to the right, narrowly avoiding an arrow.

Suddenly, he had an idea. "Colorado!" he shouted to the left and then the right. "Colorado!"

"In here," called Olympia Morelli. She was sticking her head out through one of the windows whose empty frames still remained in the livery.

Dang it, he thought. *Colorado's stove up.* One by one, they were losing their best fighters, their most experienced men.

Olympia waved at him again. "He's in here, Jason!"

He started toward her at a trot.

Matt MacDonald was up, awake, and driving Ward crazy. He was beginning to wish the Apache would break in, if only so he could take Jason's advice. At least he wouldn't have to listen to Matt's whining anymore.

And also so he'd finally have a good excuse to shoot

himself and get away from his aching shoulder. It had begun to throb and pound with a vengeance during the night.

But Matt was bound and determined to rant and rave about his lousy wife and his lousy brother-in-law and the lousy Indians. And a lot of other lousy things that Ward had managed not to listen to. Basically, he was determined to do anything but drink the secretly doctored coffee that Ward had handed him.

Again, Ward walked to the window and stared out over the town. As far as he could tell, just about everybody from town was up on the wall, including some of the women. The smoke had gone away, so he figured that the fires in the trench had finally gone out. Which left them completely open, except for the stockade.

Building the stockade hadn't been his idea. Jason was the one who'd pushed for it. And Ward remembered complaining long and loud about every log they cut up and down the creek, and hauled back and set into the ground.

Right now, though, that stockade was the best idea anybody had ever had in the whole history of everything. Ever.

The Apache must have set fire to the east end of the stockade, because men were transporting water up to the boards where other men stood, who emptied the buckets over and down the outside of the wall, then passed them back.

Ward hoped the Apache would give up on that idea fairly soon. All they had for water was the town well—well, there were some private wells, too, but the water all came from the same place. It had come back up some after the first day, but its level was going down fast once more.

But he didn't have the time to think about that at the moment. He saw Jason running across the square toward the office, and threw open the door.

"What is it?" he shouted.

"Nothin'," Jason shouted back. "Just tryin' not to get shot!"

And the second he jumped up on the boardwalk, when he was halfway through the door, an arrow caught him in the back.

Ward shouted, "Jason!" and dragged him through the door, slamming it behind him.

Oh, Jesus! Ward thought frantically as he rolled Jason's limp body on its side. *He can't die now! He can't die ever!* The arrow was high in his back, over toward the left shoulder, and it didn't seem to Ward that Jason should be dead.

But he was surely out like the proverbial light.

"Great, just great . . ." Ward grumbled.

And Matthew, whom he'd almost forgotten, said, "Splash him with water. That'll wake the bastard up."

"Shut up, Matt," Ward grumbled as he dragged Jason, dragged him with his one good arm, toward the second cell and its still unmade cot. The arrow didn't look like it was in too deep. He figured he could get it out with a yank and without having to call for the doc.

He hoped.

But first, he had to get Jason's jacket and shirt off. Which wouldn't be easy, considering. With a shake of his head, he rifled his pocket for a knife, pulled one out, and opened it. It wasn't the best, but it would do, he figured. It'd have to.

Carefully, he cut the shaft of the arrow away until only about two inches protruded from Jason's back. Then he began cutting the material of Jason's vest and shirt away in a big circle around what remained of the arrow's shaft.

"Well, I'll be damned," he said.

"Most probably," muttered Matt.

"You shut your piehole, MacDonald," snarled Ward, without wasting the time it would have taken to look up. Instead, he carefully eased the edge of his fingernail alongside the arrowhead, through the blood and tissue it had displaced. And before he had gone a quarter of an inch, slipped its edge under the side of the arrowhead.

He eased his finger—and the arrowhead—out. It released with a soft, sucking sound and rolled off Jason's back, clattering to the floor.

Ward sat frozen in disbelief, staring alternately at his hand and at the arrowhead on the floor, and at Jason's back. Now, *that* was a bloody miracle!

Ward rounded up what he could for bandages and after washing Jason's back, he tied cloth after cloth around the wound, circling Jason's shoulder and rounding his chest with the strips he'd made from tearing the thin wool blanket and the pillowcase in the cell.

Finally, he rolled Jason into what he trusted was a comfortable position, and left him alone, returning to the outer office and the desk. He didn't know how long Jason would be out, but he also didn't want to try and rush his return to consciousness.

He sat there for perhaps five minutes, then stood up with a disgusted "Damnit!"

Somebody was going to have to oversee things, and with Jason temporarily out of the picture, that somebody was him.

"Don't wake him up!" he hissed at MacDonald—whose coffee cup, he noticed, was now half-empty—and let himself out of the office and onto the street.

The noise was what hit him first, and the stench of gun smoke.

He slowly turned, looking around the town and the wall that encircled it. The inner walls were thick with the forms of both townspeople and freighters, alternately firing and reloading.

Occasionally, he saw a body drop from the scaffolding and land out of sight with a dull thud. Some of their womenfolk were still up there, too. He could see Jason's sister—Matt MacDonald's wife—and MacDonald's sister, too, as well as Mrs. Morelli and Carrie Kendall, among others.

He also spied Mayor Kendall across the way. Randall Nordstrom was on the roof of his store lying on his belly, firing his rifle out toward the south. Saul Cohen lay stretched out flat on the roof of his house and store, peppering the Apache with rifle fire.

Nordstrom and Saul gave him an idea. One he thought he might implement later, if worse came to worst.

He hoped it wouldn't.

He made his way through the town, his shoulder

plaguing him more with each step he took, each rung of
every ladder he climbed. While he was up with Jenny,
telling her about her brother's misfortune, she suddenly
shoved him aside. And arrow, headed straight for his
temple, passed him ineffectually and buried itself in her
left wrist.

Fortunately, it had passed straight through, and he was
able to break off the arrowhead and ease the shaft out the
other side. It didn't bleed much, having been high enough
up the wrist that it just passed through the fat on the outside, so he wrapped it up on the spot, using her handker-
chief for a bandage.

Jenny, the brave little thing, waved off his worries and
further ministrations—and his many thanks for saving
him—and went right back to shooting at the Apache.

"I've got eleven so far," she said. "Don't stop a lady
on a winning streak."

Truth be told, he admired Jenny, admired her a lot
more than he ought to, considering that she was the wife
of the man he currently held locked in the jail. Several
times, it had taken all the self-control he could muster
not to just haul off and shoot him.

How could somebody as nice and sweet and pretty as
Jenny stay with a worthless cow flop like Matthew Mac-
Donald? He owned the bank and everything, and Ward
supposed that he was pretty darned good-looking, if you
were a lady, but still, Jenny didn't seem the type to be
impressed by money or looks.

He shook his head. It beat everything, as far as he
could figure. But then, who could figure women?

Not him.

He took up a stance beside her for a while, getting himself three Apache while he watched her for any signs that she was about to faint or throw up or something, but when she gave no indication of that, he finally moved on. Not only was she beautiful, she was as stoic as any man.

What a girl. No. What a *woman* . . .

He found Ezra Evans and his brother, Joel, down at the southeast corner—Ezra firing east, and Joel firing south. The brothers had come with the wagon train before last, and decided to stay on. Right now, Ward was mightily glad they had, despite his off-and-on quarrels with Ezra.

Now, as he watched Ezra pick off first one mounted brave, then another, Ward decided that politics was a small thing for men to argue over.

He vowed never to do it again, at least with Ezra.

Ezra didn't see him as he climbed up, but Joel did. He held out a hand and helped him up the last step of the ladder.

"Boys need some help?" Ward asked. "Though you look to be doin' pretty good on your own. . . ."

"Help's always appreciated," replied Joel, and stepped over to make room for him.

"It's most appreciated where it's needed most," Ezra said without turning to look at him. "A man'd think these Injuns could take the hint and back the hell off," he continued, firing again. Another Indian down. "Why don't they just go home?"

"You got me," Ward said. "Seems to me we could hold off the whole of the Apache Nation with these walls. And Lord knows we got enough ammunition to last till next year."

He was lying, of course. They might have enough ammunition to last them a month or so, but they were fast running out of the men capable of using it to their advantage.

And besides that, this last ladder he'd climbed had opened up his wound again. He felt the hot blood trickling down his back and side, and a fresh, heated ache where the arrow had taken him.

He tried not to think about it, but Joel said, "Man, you're bleeding! Fresh blood!"

Ezra ducked down, pulling Ward with him, and snarled, "Idiot. You got it opened up again. I thought Jason grounded you or somethin'."

"Till he got shot," Ward answered. It was hard to talk now, although he couldn't figure why. "He's over to the office, out cold."

"You get him seen to?" Joel asked.

Weakly, Ward nodded. Suddenly he couldn't seem to find the power to move his lips, let alone speak.

"C'mon, Joel," Ward heard Ezra say. "Let's get him down to the doc. He's losin' a lot of blood."

There might have been further conversation, but Ward didn't hear it.

He passed out.

The wagon train

Blake called a halt early, and the men began to gather wood while the women got together the ingredients for the supper they would make. Becky Mankiller had her 'em to gather what precious things they got. None of this may be here when we come back. And wake Ezekial and Eliza, too. I'll get the horses."

"Don't you think you better get dressed first?" Jason asked, pointing at Zachary's nightdress and the scarf wrapped round his chin to protect his long gray beard.

This forced a quick grin from Zachary at last. "Aye, thank you, Jason. Be with you in a minute."

The door slammed between them.

Ward, standing near Jason, sniffed.

And Jason said, "Right. Ward, take some of these men and hitch up the Mortons' two wagons. Let out their cattle and goats while you're at it, and chase 'em off to the hills up northeast."

"Zachary ain't gonna be happy," Jason heard Ward mutter as he walked off.

Well, Zach'll be happier rounding them up again than finding them butchered, Jason thought with justification. Zachary could be a tough old bird, but he had a sound mind and a good heart.

By the time Ward drove up the first wagon, Ezekial and Eliza was coming out the front door, and hustling Electa and Europa between them. Both Electa and her sister Europa—the widow of Milton Griggs, who was to be the town's blacksmith—carried armloads of schoolbooks, for both Morton girls taught school in town. Their mother, Eliza, carried a large paper globe in addition to a box of what Jason assumed were her treasures.

The second wagon came up straightaway, and Jason saw Zachary and Susannah up into it. Zachary had brought a rifle and a case full of gunsmithing tools, heart set on a rich rabbit stew, and Olin's wife agreed with her.

But the men brought back three grouse and a black snake—not hearty fare for a party of their size—so Laura Blake broke out the last of their bacon. That, along with the wild game, made a passable meal when combined with the copious cornbread that Becky baked up and served with the wild honey they'd found a few days back.

In fact, the Whaler boys ate an entire pan by themselves, and started on a second.

Later, after the dishes were done, the last coffee drunk, and everyone was in bed, Laura curled against Blake's side and whispered, "It was gone today, wasn't it? There wasn't any more."

"Wasn't any more of what?"

"The smoke on the horizon."

He turned his head, lifting his eyebrows at her.

"We may be women, but that doesn't make us stupid, you know."

He blinked rapidly, but she didn't give him time to reply.

"I saw the smoke, and so did Becky. And I woke early. There was more this morning, before the dawn."

"And how could you see it if it was before the dawn?"

"The smoke was very dark and much thicker than before. Opaque. The moonlight was enough to see by."

Blake was silent for a moment. Then he said, "It could be several things, Laura. It could be a wildfire."

"It could be Fury. Fury burning."

"It's better not to worry your head, my dear," he said soothingly, although he knew her concerns were well founded. It had been preying on his mind since yesterday.

He added, "We'll find out soon enough. And I'm sure it's nothing, nothing at all. Now, go to sleep. Dawn comes quickly."

He whispered a quiet prayer, and was not surprised when she echoed his "Amen."

13

At about five that afternoon, about the same time that Blake and his travelers were sitting down to stew and cornbread, Doc Morelli stopped by Cohen's Hardware. He wanted to check on Rachael Cohen, and perhaps change her bandages if need be.

He found her—and her boys—still tucked into the store's first-floor storage room. Saul, she told him, was somewhere up on the wall.

She was doing well, very well, in fact, for having just lost a baby after a difficult delivery. Perhaps it was her good spirits and her faith in her husband that kept her going. Surely the constant sounds of shouting and gunfire couldn't be doing her any good.

With this in mind, he left her with a paper filled with sleeping powders. "Take half of this if you need it," he said as he handed it to her. "And the other half's for later. It'll make you sleep."

She took the paper, but set it on the bed stand without looking at it. "Thank you, Dr. Morelli, but I'd rather stay awake to worry about my husband. And watch these naughty boys of mine." She smiled thinly.

"I just saw Saul," said Morelli with a nod. "He's a very brave man, Rachael."

"Thank you," she murmured. "I know."

He stood up and lifted his medical bag. "If there's nothing else then, I'm needed back at the hospital. The livery stables, I should say." Casualties were growing by the hour, and he only took comfort in the fact that the afternoon was almost over and that night would soon be upon them.

"Thank you for stopping by," Rachael said again. "My prayers are with the fighting men."

"And I'm certain they're appreciating them, ma'am," he replied as he let himself out into the store.

Once he was outside, he was pleased to see that the gates still held, and also happy to hear that the incidence of gunfire seemed to have slackened off. As had the number of stray arrows and spears sailing over the stockade.

Were the Indians backing off for the day already? It seemed too early, but if they wanted to take the time off, he was more than happy to grant it to them.

Although his primary objective was the stable, he dropped his bag inside the door. Then he made his way around the building and up to the scaffolding on the interior of the stockade.

Carefully, he inched his way around the bodies of the men still fighting as he moved toward Saul Cohen.

"Dr. Morelli?" Saul said, surprised. "Is it my Rachael? Is something—"

"No, no, Saul, nothing's wrong."

Saul signaled to him, and they both crouched down below the jagged opening of hand-hewn spikes at the top of the stockade. "You've seen her then?" Saul asked.

"Yes, and she's doing quite well. I left some sleeping powder with her, which she refused to take. I gather she'd rather worry about you."

Saul ducked his head and chuckled.

"Tonight, you make sure she takes a dose, all right?" said Morelli. "She needs the sleep."

Saul nodded in the affirmative. "I will be certain."

"Is it just my imagination, or are the Indians actually going away?"

Saul shrugged. "Your guess is as good as mine, Doctor. For all I know, they may be planning to sing us to sleep, then sneak in and murder us all with the coda."

Saul had lost Morelli somewhere along the way, but he nodded just the same and said, "I've got to see to the men in the livery now, Saul. Take care of yourself."

The doctor turned and carefully made his way back to the ladder.

Jenny hugged the stockade to allow the doctor to pass, and Megan did the same. When he disappeared down the ladder, Jenny said, "What do you think they're up to? I haven't had a decent target in over ten minutes. You don't think they're actually . . . quitting?"

"You mean turning tail? Heading for the hills?" Megan sneered. "Hardly. I mean, there's still some light left to die by!"

"But then again, Jason always says that you can't out-guess an Apache," Jenny muttered.

Megan sighed. "He's right about that, I'd say."

Jenny looked at her flatly, her pent-up anger at last finding an escape. "You said it was right that I marry your brother, too."

"That was a long time ago," Megan snapped, but then thought better of it. "Sorry, Jen. It was just that you seemed, I mean, the both of you seemed . . . Things were different."

"I think they just seemed different." Jenny stood higher and took another peek over the stockade. There were no Apache in sight right now. She ducked back down and plucked nervously at the bandage on her wrist.

"I think that Matt just made things seem different because he wanted to marry me," she said. "And not for my sake. I think he just wanted to show my brother that he could do whatever he wished, you know?"

Megan remained silent.

"And he surely showed him, didn't he?" Jenny added with a shake of her head.

"Don't beat yourself up over it, baby," Megan said kindly. "You were young and in love. People have done far worse things for only one of those reasons."

"But not here and not now, and not to my brother," Jenny replied. "I do love Jason, Megan. Love him more than anything or anyone else. He's my blood."

Megan knew exactly what she meant, but kept it to herself.

Instead, she said, "Jason's your brother, Jenny. Of course you care for him. But it's different when it's somebody else. Somebody like Matt. Oh, rats," she swore softly, her cheeks flushed beneath the freckles. "Well, you know what I mean. How's your wrist?"

"Fine, thanks. Smarts a little, but what can a person expect?" Jenny stared at the plank under her feet. "I'll make it up to Jason somehow. Somehow, I promise I will."

Megan cocked her fist against her hip. "And you'll leave me to clean up after Matt?"

Jenny couldn't help but laugh. "Clean up after him? He's housebroken at least!"

Megan sniffed. "Barely."

On both sides of them, men were climbing or skidding down the ladders. They'd given up on Indian-fighting for the evening, it seemed. But the girls held their posts, if only because of the conversation in which they were engaged.

Jenny sobered a little. "Megan, I'm sorry. I'm sorry because he's your brother, and I know I shouldn't speak ill of him in front of you."

But Megan only waved a hand. "Speak ill all you want. He's a rotten sonofabitch, and I know it. It's just the way things are."

"Megan!"

"Oh, Jenny. You sound like you're surprised. You've heard us fight. You've heard me call him far worse, and to his face."

Jenny had.

But still, she thought there must be love behind it. She and Jason had argued, too, although not so fiercely as the MacDonald siblings, but there was always love behind it. And no matter what Megan said, she'd never believe that she didn't really, down deep, love her very own brother.

"All right, Megan," she said softly, hoping to end the conversation. For the present anyway.

"You're not getting off that easy, Jenny," Megan said, although there was a hint of a smile on her wide lips. She rose up, glanced out through the stockade spikes, then said, "We'll talk about this later, but right now, I want to get myself a—"

Out of nowhere, an Apache arrow sank into her neck. She toppled from the stockade.

"Megan!" sobbed Jenny, rushing down the ladder after her fallen friend. "Megan! Help! Dr. Morelli!"

Over at the jail, Jason was just coming to.

The first thing he noticed was that Matt MacDonald was sleeping, judging by the soft, rhythmic snores coming from the next cell. The second thing he noticed was that his shoulder hurt. Not much, but enough that he felt a sharp, smarting pinch when he tried to sit up. And he seemed to have been bandaged by a one-armed, near-sighted monkey. With his blanket!

Or at least, pieces of it.

He managed to swing himself up into a sitting position, then lever himself up to stand. None of it was easy, considering how he was wrapped up. As soon as he found his hat, he was going to find Doc Morelli and let him sort it out.

He had his hat on and was clear out the door before

he realized that the sound of gunfire was distinctly absent from the air. That stopped him in his tracks.

Also, the men from the wagons circling the town square were gathered around the big campfire where Olympia Morelli, bless her heart, was overseeing the turning of a big spit on which was skewered a sizzling side of beef.

Rollie Biggston, still swathed in bandages, was open for business and standing out in the street, hawking his wares to the crowd. Abigail Krimp could be seen through the windows, behind the bar, dressed in bright blue shiny satin, pulling and serving drinks as fast as she could to the wall-to-wall crowd.

It wasn't quite dark, yet there was no one up on the walls that he could see. No sounds of gunfire, no signs of flying arrows or Apache trying to climb the walls or set the stockade on fire.

Something was wrong.

But he didn't have time to think about it, because just then he heard his name shouted frantically. Doc Morelli shouted again and waved at him from the livery.

He took off at a dead run, and reached Morelli's side in a matter of seconds. "What is it?" he panted. "What's wrong?"

Jenny burst from behind the doctor and threw her arms about Jason. "It's my fault, my fault, Jason," she sobbed into his chest.

"No, it isn't, Jenny," said Morelli before his eyes flicked to Jason's. "It's Megan. She's hurt."

Carefully but purposefully, Jason peeled Jenny from his chest and moved past her, following Morelli back through the stable. There, on a small white cot, lay his girl. Her neck was bandaged, and the bandages were soaked with blood and fluid.

His legs suddenly felt like jelly, and he sat down on the edge of her cot without willing it. "Megan," he whispered. "Megan . . ." He lifted her hand to his lips and brushed a kiss over it. She didn't wake.

He lifted his gaze to Morelli. "Will she . . . I mean, is she going to . . ." He couldn't say it, couldn't verbalize it. It was too important a question for anyone to ask.

But apparently not too difficult to answer. Morelli said, "Hard to tell right now, but I think she'll make it, Jason. She's as hard to kill as you are. And don't even think about going anywhere until I get a chance to take those old wool bandages off you, take a good look and clean the wound, and then get you wrapped in some good, clean cotton swathing."

"Right," Jason said softly. He had eyes for no one but Megan right now, and no feelings except those for Megan and the girl who clung to his side. His little Jenny, his little sister.

How had everything turned out so wrong? Why did his father have to die not even halfway here, the victim of a Comanche arrow? Why did they have to settle here, in what appeared to be Apache and bandit country?

And why did Matt's father have to be the one to tumble down a mountainside to his death, when it could just as easily have been Matt? Jason figured that old Hamish wouldn't have been nearly as much trouble to contend with as his spoiled son.

Course, things always worked out better in hindsight, didn't they?

Eventually, Dr. Morelli wheeled over a makeshift cart with bandages and ointments and so on, and began to go to work on Jason's wound, such as it was. "Hardly grazed you," the doctor said, and Jason was glad.

He unwrapped a good half-blanket's worth of dressing from Jason's shoulder—which Jason had to admit made moving much easier.

Then he made Jason take off his vest and shirt—cut full of holes though they were—so that he could carefully wash and medicate his wound.

Then he rebandaged Jason with a quarter of the material he'd been originally strapped with. This time, however, the dressing was soft, clean, cotton bandages instead of the scratchy wool stuff.

And lastly, despite Jason's rather vigorous protests to the contrary, Doc gave him a dose of laudanum, putting him down for the count.

14

Lone Wolf carved another thick slice off the roasting carcass of the cow his scouts had brought in. He had already assigned the three horses to braves whose mounts had been shot from beneath them, and they had finished eating the ducks hours ago.

It was now past sunset, and all he could see of the town was a flicker of light through the stockade.

He had called his men back early. They were taking far too many casualties compared to the whites he saw dropping from the walls. At first he thought that perhaps he and his warriors were beaten, and that they should just go home.

But that would be a bad thing—to go home empty-handed, and with so many wounded, so many dead. He remembered a farm—a large one—he had seen while scouting up north of the town last season. It was a farm with many cattle and goats that they could drive off, and what men he had seen were old. Very old.

He was thinking that perhaps they would ride north in the morning, all of them. They would kill these settlers and take their livestock. It would be simple, for there were only the two old men and a few women, two of them young enough for his braves to take some pleasure with.

Plus, riding to the north might bring the townspeople out of their fortress and into the open. More than anything, he wanted them in the open, where his men could see to shoot and where they might take trophies: jewelry, watches, shirts, hands, private parts, and many horses and cattle.

"Tell the men to sleep well," he said to the brave next to him. "Tomorrow we ride north. There will be a battle, of this I am certain, and it will be fairly matched. Tell them."

While the brave nodded and ran to tell the next knot of warriors the news, Lone Wolf grunted.

Tomorrow would be better.

Tomorrow they would ride on the wings of the eagle, and make war with an enemy who did not hide behind walls made of pointed logs.

Tomorrow they would be victorious.

Saul sat at home, at his wife's bedside, while his boys played checkers on the floor. He had talked about his day, although he had left out the more grisly parts—not only because he didn't want the boys to hear, but because he didn't wish to put more worry on his Rachael than necessary. He felt that she was very fragile now, and was hardly up to hearing the details.

He had made their dinner, and now he gathered up

the plates and silverware and carried them upstairs to wash later. Under the circumstances, he felt no need to rush things.

But halfway up the stairs, he stopped stock still. They hadn't heard a word from the Mortons for days! Someone should ride up there. Someone should ride up and bring them into town.

But who?

Most of the town's good men were down for the moment. Some of their good men were dead, if the truth be told. He thought of Gil Collins, who they thought had died once before, not long after they settled in Fury, but who'd rallied and come back, only to be injured again by this most recent batch of Apache cutthroats.

Batch? It was a whole army!

And cutthroats was too kind a word.

He forced himself to move again, and told himself he mustn't think about the Morton clan.

He made it clear to the top of the stairs before he stopped again, and then he went to the sink. He stood there a long time, his hands balancing his weight on the edge of the sink, his head down.

He detested moral dilemmas. They made his head hurt, and his stomach, too. But then he realized that he didn't have to go through all this inner struggle. Why should the business of the town be the problem of a mere shop owner?

Jason! This should be something for the sheriff to decide, shouldn't it?

Of course it should! A great burden was suddenly lifted from his shoulders, and he practically jogged down the steps, stuck his head in the back room long enough to say, "I'll be back in a few minutes, Rachael," and scooted out the front door.

It took him several stops to locate Jason, but he finally found him at the livery, arguing with Doc Morelli. Over the stew, of all things.

"We keep this up, we're gonna run out of beef to slaughter," Jason was saying as Saul came up. He said it with a faint slur, as if the doctor had given him medication he was fighting off the last dregs of. He was bandaged across his chest and shoulder.

"Saul!" Jason said, and smiled. Saul thought it remarkable that he didn't even wince, even though he wasn't on a cot. He was sitting next to one, as if he'd been in conversation with the occupant. He continued. "What can I do for you?"

Saul told him about his fears for the Mortons. And when he was finished, he shrugged and added, "Well, you asked. I just told it."

"And you were right," Jason said. He leaned down over the cot, whispered something that Saul couldn't hear, then lifted the hand of the woman—he could tell she was a woman at least—and kissed it.

"Is it his sister?" Saul asked the doctor in a whisper.

"No, it's Megan MacDonald," said Morelli. "Caught an arrow in the neck," he added, softer still.

Saul thought he must have made a face, because Morelli added quickly, "It's not so bad as you might think. Jason knows this."

As if that would help, Saul thought. He had been reassured again and again that Rachael would be all right, but that didn't stop him from thinking about her, worrying about her constantly.

Jason stood up, and it was then that Saul saw Jenny was there, too, standing behind him in the shadows. "Don't worry, Jason," said Morelli, "I'll stay with her."

Jason nodded, and asked for his shirt.

But Jenny waved Morelli off. "Don't put that filthy thing on again, Jason. Stop by the house and pick up something fresh."

"All right, Boss," Jason said, and pulled her close enough to kiss her forehead. "Won't be long. Thanks, Doc."

Morelli nodded in acknowledgment, and before he knew it, Saul was on the street with Jason, walking up toward Jason's house.

It took only a minute before Jason came out of his bedroom, wearing a fresh shirt and vest, and pinned on his badge again, then started down toward the center of town again. Saul tagged at his heels like a puppy.

Jason stopped in mid-step, startling him, and said, "Go home, Saul. This is my job."

As much as Saul wanted to do just that, he said, "But Jason—"

"No. I'm going to need to take some good men with me, but I'm also going to need to leave some good men here in town. Got me?"

A moment passed before Saul said, "Yes, Jason. I understand."

"Get going then, buddy."

Saul trotted happily back down the street, toward his hardware store and his family.

* * *

Jason rounded up ten men, including himself and Ward Wanamaker and a number of the wagon drivers. They spoke with the other settlers and learned that the northern attack force had withdrawn around the wall to camp with those on the south.

Jason was relieved to hear this. The last thing he needed, to his mind, was to have to fight his way out of the town, and then back into it. He was counting on the Apache being asleep for this little foray.

They eased open the gate and exited the town single file, with Jason on his best mare, Cleo. She stood out in the moonlight, her golden palomino coloring glistening with reflected moonbeams, so Jason kept to the inside of the pack.

Once they left the fortress town behind them and were a mile in the clear, they goosed their horses into a canter. It was light enough to see, and they reached the Morton farm in good time.

Jason beat on the door until it was opened by old Zachary Morton. Or rather, the barrel of his gun. "What the hell you doin' out here, Jason, wakin' honest folks in the middle of the night?" The door opened a little wider to reveal his wife Susannah at his side.

"Mrs. Morton," Jason said, tipping his hat. "We came to get you folks and take you into town. We've been beset by Apache, and I got a feeling they'll be headed this way next since they can't get past our walls."

"We been seein' the smoke rise," Zachary said, his features hardening. "Susannah, go wake the gals an' tell 'em to gather what precious things they got. None of this may be here when we come back. And wake Ezekial and Eliza, too. I'll get the horses."

"Don't you think you better get dressed first?" Jason asked, pointing at Zachary's nightdress and the scarf wrapped round his chin to protect his long gray beard.

This forced a quick grin from Zachary at last. "Aye, thank you, Jason. Be with you in a minute."

The door slammed between them.

Ward, standing near Jason, sniffed.

And Jason said, "Right. Ward, take some of these men and hitch up the Mortons' two wagons. Let out their cattle and goats while you're at it, and chase 'em off to the hills up northeast."

"Zachary ain't gonna be happy," Jason heard Ward mutter as he walked off.

Well, Zach'll be happier rounding them up again than finding them butchered, Jason thought with justification. Zachary could be a tough old bird, but he had a sound mind and a good heart.

By the time Ward drove up the first wagon, Ezekial and Eliza was coming out the front door, and hustling Electa and Europa between them. Both Electa and her sister Europa—the widow of Milton Griggs, who was to be the town's blacksmith—carried armloads of schoolbooks, for both Morton girls taught school in town. Their mother, Eliza, carried a large paper globe in addition to a box of what Jason assumed were her treasures.

The second wagon came up straightaway, and Jason saw Zachary and Susannah up into it. Zachary had brought a rifle and a case full of gunsmithing tools,

Jason supposed, and Susannah carried the fry pans and roaster and knives and loaf pans temporarily wrapped in dresses and bed linens and layers of raw yard goods. Behind him in the dark, Jason heard their livestock being herded away from the ranch, heard them picking up speed as they headed north.

Farm, he corrected himself, *not ranch.* The Mortons always called it their farm.

Well, they did grow their own hay and grain in the irrigated fields west of the house and barn, along the riverbank. He'd give them that.

Mostly, though, what they were interested in was livestock. His men were presently herding off some nice Angora goats, along with the last of the Morgans that Matt MacDonald's father had brought out, and which Matt didn't seem to want. Zachary had confided in Jason that he'd bought them cheap.

Most of the Morton's draft mares were pulling their wagons, and two had foals frisking at their sides. There were about a dozen head of cattle, and the men were driving off the hogs, too. He thought they had about fifteen, plus whatever litters they'd dropped this spring. There were the mules and the saddle horses, too, followed by their big old dog, his tail wagging at the chance to do some unscheduled work.

Jason hoped they could run them out far enough that the Apache didn't catch them. Mostly because he hated the smell of roasting mule, and he knew that was what the Apache would do right away.

To celebrate their victory, that is.

"Move out!" he called, and the wagons slowly began

to move south. He knew the men moving the livestock would catch up in no time, once the livestock was safely hidden.

And they did, after the main group had made five miles.

"You get 'em far away?" Jason asked.

The men nodded that they had.

"Found a little box canyon about seven or eight miles from the ranch," said Dusty Carmichael, another who had come to Fury with the freighter wagons. "Got 'em all settled in there right and proper, and left the dog to watch over 'em."

"Good," Jason said.

The Mortons' dog, called Old Chunk, was a very large and mostly white conglomeration of herding breeds. And he didn't just herd anything you told him to. No sir, he protected those critters like they were his own puppies. No wolves or coyotes or cougars—not even a grizzly bear—would dare to bother them with Old Chunk around.

The wagons and riders picked up some speed. They had only two miles to go before they made town.

15

About a mile from town, they were riding at a trot when Jason heard Ward holler, "Damn it! Pick a new place!" And the shout was followed by a burst of gunfire and pounding hooves.

Jason galloped up to the front of the line, where Ward had been traveling, and found him still sitting his horse, but with a new arrow jutting from his shoulder. "I swan, Jason, have I got some sorta target painted on me or somethin'?"

About five of the men had ridden out after the lone brave who'd fired the arrow, so Jason helped Ward down from his horse and into the back of one of the Mortons' wagons—the one with only two Mortons in it.

"Ain't you gonna get the arrow out?" Ward called after him.

"No, gonna leave it for Doc Morelli. Treating you is one of his favorite pastimes."

"Aw, beans!"

Jason tied Ward's horse's reins to the back of the wagon while Ward continued to complain, and at last the men who'd ridden out galloped back in. Jason didn't ask them whether they'd caught their prey. The fresh blood spraying from the hair grasped in one rider's hand was all the answer he needed.

"All right, settle down," was all Jason said. "We're gonna ride fast for the two gate, got it?"

Ride fast, they did. They made such a rattle and racket that they found the gates open for them, and closed up right behind. Poor old Eliza was bounced halfway from her seat by the time they got the horses stopped.

From there on out, Ezekial said that that was the ride that did his Eliza in. She had a minor stroke sometime while they were on their last, frantic gallop into town, Doc Morelli later said, and thereafter got around on one crutch.

Jason had the men park the wagons out back of his house, near the corral, and gave shelter to the Mortons in his home. He had three bedrooms—one for him, one for Jenny, and the third they had built on in memory of his father. The Morton crew filled them up just fine.

Of course, Jenny would have to sleep on the couch. If she slept at all.

He sort of doubted she'd leave Megan's side, though. Those two were thicker than thieves.

After thanking the men and seeing Ward off to the doctor (and looking in on Megan, who was asleep, along with Jenny in the chair beside her bed), he took himself over to the office.

Matt was still sleeping. Jason thought that Matt ought to thank his lucky stars that he was sleeping so much from the dope Dr. Morelli was providing for him. Otherwise, he'd most likely be dead and it'd be Jason locked behind those bars, sleeping on that cot.

Of course, he'd been sleeping on a twin to Matt's cot for the last few nights anyway. Might as well make it official.

He stopped himself just before he pulled the trigger. He didn't even remember pulling his sidearm, didn't remember aiming it. He did remember the overwhelming glee he felt when his finger rode the trigger and the gun was aimed at Matthew's skull, however—followed immediately by a sharp rush of guilt.

That was generally the way it was when it came to his relationship with Matt: It teetered precariously between culpable loathing and downright, abject hatred. Lately, the last one was winning out.

Quite a bit more than he would have liked.

He didn't want to hate Matt. He didn't want to hate anybody, except maybe some of those Apache out there right now. But he especially hadn't wanted to hate his sister's husband, let alone the brother of his intended bride.

Jenny was leaving him now, though. Which was almost like giving Jason permission to hate him.

Well, not really.

God wasn't *that* good.

He slumped down in the chair behind the desk and looked up at the clock. Ten thirty-three. Word ought to be getting around by now about the Mortons, and what that meant. He slowly looked out and over the town.

Lamplight began to glow behind formerly darkened windows.

News was traveling, all right.

But he was beat. He found himself falling asleep where he sat, and made himself stand up and walk to the empty cell.

Two minutes after lying down on the cot and tossing his hat aside, he was asleep and dreaming of a life back East, a life filled with school and books and clean clothing and steady meals.

And no Apache.

Across the plaza inside the livery stable, Jenny sat, crouched next to Megan's bed, half-asleep under the watchful eye of Doc Morelli.

Megan was resting easier now, and he hoped she'd continue to do so. The arrow had done terrible internal damage, but Jenny had gotten her here quickly, and he'd stitched her up the best he knew how. Now she was in God's hands, and her own. If she didn't jerk out the stitches, she'd make it.

Morelli understood from Jason that Jenny had made the decision to leave her husband. He hadn't said anything, but he was happy for her. He could hardly bear to be in the same town with the man for ten minutes. He couldn't imagine what it was like for Jenny to live with him.

Poor little thing.

Both Megan and Jenny, that is. They were very much alike. And Jason loved the both of them. He wondered why Jason hadn't wed Megan long ago. They were made for each other—this was clear. Perhaps it was that she was a MacDonald.

Morelli could see where that might be a stopping point for someone like Jason.

But still, he didn't see why it should keep them apart now. They could still have holidays without inviting Matthew to the table.

He smiled at himself a little.

His eyes went to his newest patient, Ward Wanamaker. Three separate times he'd had to patch that man up in less than four days! Or was it three? Five? Quite honestly, he had lost count. He hadn't slept, outside of an occasional stolen ten minutes here or a half hour there, and the days and nights were all running together.

Anyway, he'd doped the deputy as much as he thought was safe, dug the arrowhead out as carefully as he could, stitched up the wound, and said good night. Ward was feeling no pain at the moment, but tomorrow he'd be feeling it and he'd be a bear.

Morelli wasn't looking forward to the coming day.

Lone Wolf had sent out two braves to look for Hawk Fingers when he didn't come back on time, and after he'd heard shots from far away in the direction that Hawk Fingers had ridden. And he was saddened to see them finally riding back at a slow jog with the pony of Hawk Fingers between them and with Hawk Fingers, blood covering his hairless, scalped head and trailing slowly down his pony's side, strapped over it.

"Who has done this thing?" asked Cunning Dog, who had just walked up beside Lone Wolf. Cunning Dog had led the party of men who had brought him three riding horses, along with the cow and the ducks they had just eaten. "The whites? The Yuma?"

Lone Wolf assumed he'd included the Yuma because Hawk Fingers had been scalped.

White men did not scalp, in their experience.

Lone Wolf had already decided that their experience with the whites was about to change.

"Whites," he said, scowling as if the taste of the word was like offal in his mouth.

"What will we do?" asked Cunning Dog.

He nodded toward the braves who had brought back the body. "They will see to Hawk Fingers. You, come to my fire. We will talk."

Cunning Dog followed him curiously, but Lone Wolf had already made up his mind as to the course of their next actions.

The whites would be sorry they had taken the lives of so many good Apache warriors. They would be sorry for those they had lamed and wounded and mutilated.

Lone Wolf planned to make them sorry they were ever born, had ever traveled west.

They would die screaming.

Several beds away from where Dr. Morelli sat dozing, Ward Wanamaker dreamt.

He dreamt of when he was a small boy, back on his daddy's farm in Maryland. They had cows and chickens and ducks and sheep and horses, too, and his favorite was a black pony named Flint.

In his dream, he held out his hand, offering a lump of sugar, and Flint came up to the fence, faster than ever before, and took it from him.

He reached out to touch Flint, his feet off the ground, his belly seesawing on the middle board of the fence his father had built, when Flint suddenly turned on him, latching his teeth onto the boy's sleeve and yanking him forward.

He screamed, he thought, as the pony's front feet came down again and again on his shoulder, then his back. And then he couldn't scream anymore.

He heard his father cry, "Ward, I told you to stay away from those damn Apache!" and heard his father's running footsteps coming closer, bringing salvation with them.

But it was too late. In his dream, he was already dead, his small shoulder and thin back crushed and bloodied by tiny, sharp black hooves.

He slept on, but not so peacefully as before.

Over at the sheriff's house, the Mortons slept fitfully, if only because they were not in their own beds. Zachary and Ezekial both tossed and turned, worried about their livestock, worried about their home and their crops.

Their wives, Susannah and Eliza, slept deeper than they did, but still fretted in their dreams, concerned about their kitchens and their families, and what tomorrow might bring. Eliza fretted less than Susannah, benumbed by her stroke, although it had been small. Her right arm had gone completely numb, and she would walk into walls, walk to her right, for weeks afterward. And she would forever use a crutch.

Dr. Morelli had come to the house to see her, and promised that she would be all right in time. All things healed in time, according to him. And for the time being, he'd brought her a pair of crutches.

Zachary and Susannah's girls, Electa and Europa, were restless in general.

Europa had dreams of her late husband's death and Electa dreamed of the children in their school, dreamt of the Apache storming in and killing them all most gruesomely. And they both dreamed of their poor Aunt Eliza, crippled for no good reason.

Both girls—not girls now, but grown woman in their thirties, one an old maid and one a widow—cried fitfully in their sleep.

At around four-thirty in the morning, the Apache, led by Lone Wolf, began to make a slowly circuitous trip around the outskirts of the town, headed north toward the large farm Lone Wolf had spotted there sometime ago.

Although their numbers were greatly diminished since the start of the fight, Lone Wolf's men traveled silently and steadily, and soon they had put the town behind them. They were more than one hundred in number, having left the wounded behind, as well as a small force to attack the south side of the settlement in the morning.

He wanted the north side of the town to think it was safe. He wanted them to send a force north, toward the flames and smoke of the buildings the Apache would burn.

He would wait until first light to attack. The smoke couldn't be seen by the town at night.

And he wanted it to be seen.

He wondered if he and his men could hurt the farm

people enough so that they might be heard from the town.

He doubted it, but they would try anyway.

He spoke to the man at his left, instructing him to drop out at the side of the trail. He was to wait nearby and to signal the next man when the whites were on the way. Another mile, and he dropped off another man with the same instructions, and so on and so on.

At last, he sighted the Morton farm, its large, well-constructed buildings picked out by the first feeble rays of the rising sun.

He sent his men out to secrete themselves behind crops, behind bushes, and behind rocks. He sent them to scatter their ponies behind the hill to the west.

All men were armed with the weapons of silence—the arrow, the spear, the ax, the knife. They would wait for his signal to attack.

16

Morning came early.

At the same time the Apache attacked the Morton home and found it empty, the remainder of the Indians were attacking the walls of Fury.

Those attacking Fury had little luck. Their numbers were few, and the men on the walls mowed them down without mercy. The truth was that the whites were tired and angry: tired of the constant onslaught and the interruption of their daily routines, and angry that the Apache had had the unmitigated nerve to attack them in the first place.

And the braves at the Mortons'? They found no one, not one person, not one head of livestock, nothing. All they found was a few buildings to burn and some crops, but the crops were too young and green to catch fire, and there was no one inside the flaming buildings to scream out.

It was a failure, no matter how you looked at it.

And Lone Wolf was not one to look on the sunny side of anything.

They burned the house and the outbuildings, including the fine barn the brothers had worked so hard to complete, along with its store of baled hay and straw and bins of oats and corn. They destroyed everything they could to show that a white had ever lived there, had ever thought of living there, or even thought of daring to pass by.

Lone Wolf gained some degree of satisfaction from this, but not all he could have. There was no word from his scouts that the people from the town were on their way. Obviously, whoever lived here had been taken into the town, along with their livestock, before Lone Wolf thought to send someone to watch the way.

Forgive me, Hawk Fingers, he thought.

There had been more than enough time for the town to notice their smoke. More than enough time for them to send help to the farm, if they were going to send it at all. *And they are not,* he decided.

He signaled for his braves' attention, and then he stepped up on a large rock. "The whites have tricked us, shamed us, my brothers. We have burned their buildings, but the people and animals are gone."

"They probably fled to the town last night, and that is why Hawk Fingers is dead," called a voice from the crowd.

Lone Wolf continued. "That is correct. We will go back and attack the town from the north side, and aid our brothers who storm it from the south."

Then he raised his battle ax into the air and screamed out a war cry. This was echoed by the braves about him before they scattered toward the hill over which they'd left their ponies.

"Tonight we will dance on their bones," he muttered in a tone both determined and icy. "For today they will all perish, to the last dog and tiniest child."

Jason found himself up on the stockade wall again, but facing easier odds than he had ever imagined. The boys on the north and east walls reported no action. Nothing at all. And so most of them, leaving a few sentries behind, had joined in the fight to the south.

By eight o'clock that morning, they had no one left to fight.

But Jason was still worried. He supposed the rest of their force might have gone north with the intention of sacking the Morton place, though. And when a cry came that there was smoke on the northern horizon, he knew it for a fact. He only prayed that the livestock had been driven far enough away that they wouldn't find them.

And he didn't suppose they had, because next came the call that a cloud of dust was coming toward them from the north—dust on the road to the Morton farm.

He left a few men on the south wall—the Apache would likely circle them, he knew—but he wanted to get in the best possible volley when they reached the north side. He wanted to shock them into going away and never coming back, if possible.

To tell the truth, it was beyond him why the Apache had picked this particular time to attack them anyway. They hadn't trespassed on Apache Territory, the crops were too young to steal, they still didn't have much in the way of livestock—except for cats, that is—the

He would have gone on home, if he were in their oes. Or in their moccasins, if you wanted to put a ally fine point on it. Which, he supposed, Milcher ould. It occurred to him that he hadn't seen hide nor air of the reverend since the first day of the attack, and ven then Milcher was running away, shooing his family efore him like a frightened flock of goslings.

Somebody ought to paint a big, fat, yellow stripe down his back, that's what.

Didn't he believe in "an eye for an eye, a tooth for a tooth"?

Some man of God he was.

Ward finished reloading his six-shooter and slowly rose up again, carefully aiming his weapon at one particular brave who was sneaking too close.

A steady pull on the trigger, and the brave moved no more.

Why didn't they just give up? There couldn't be more than twenty or twenty-five braves attacking on the south. And why the hell hadn't one of the forts seen the smoke and sent their troops to come rushing in?

No, he corrected himself. The forts were too far off o have seen any smoke, even that big, black billow that vent up from the oil. Fury was located on a boil on the ackside of the devil's butt, that was for sure, and obody was looking out for them but Jason.

And maybe God.

Although God wasn't doing an awful good job of ately.

He trained his sights on yet another brave, and downed in no time. Then one other, which he figured he'd at

Milchers' mother cat, along with her get, had been on a kitten-making binge ever since they got to Fury—but he didn't think the Apache were fond of them.

Also, they weren't blocking the stream of water that he knew ran down through Apache Territory. And they certainly weren't depleting the herds of pronghorn antelope the Apache relied upon to feed them. Oh, they shot one every once in a while, but so far they'd been able to survive on their own goats, hogs, sheep, cattle, ducks, and chickens. They prided themselves on being a self-sufficient lot.

So what had gotten into these blasted Apaches? He'd be damned if he knew. All that was certain was that they'd better have a good reason for killing all these men in a battle—a battle that he fervently hoped they would never win.

He stopped by his house to tell the Morton men what was going on—and that they'd probably lost their buildings—but Eliza haltingly informed him that their men had picked up their arms and were gone.

"The rest of us can fight, too, you know," she said defensively, if shakenly. Jason guessed that there'd been a little row about it before he got there that had displaced her more than the small apoplexy Doc Morelli had reported she'd suffered.

"I thank you, Eliza," he said, "and I'll keep it in mind. But for the time being, you can be the most help by staying inside and staying down, all right?"

She nodded grudgingly—if a little to the right—and he hightailed it to the wall before she could let loose with anything else.

Mayor Kendall was still standing, Jason noticed as he climbed up the stockade ladder, and he had taken up a position about thirty feet down the wall. Saul Cohen was up and at 'em, too. Jason saw Ezra and Joel Evans down the way, and several of the wagon drivers from the convoy camped in the center of town, including Treat Paris and Jesse Figg and their leader, Fred Barlow. But they were far fewer in number than when they had started out, and Jason's hope for a good outcome began to shrink.

They still couldn't see anything but dust coming from the north, but the cloud was getting bigger by the second. Somebody down the line fired, and Jason automatically yelled at him to hold on. "Stop wasting ammunition!" he hollered.

And then a shot rang out from the oncoming Indian storm. He didn't know where they had picked up a firearm, but he hoped they knew even less about it than that shot indicated.

Maybe yes, maybe no. But he saw the slug sink into the ground with a puff of dust about thirty feet out from the trench.

They were closer than he'd thought.

He shouted, "Everybody, fire at will!" after counting to five. They still couldn't see any braves for the dust cloud, but by now, their slugs should reach into the approaching pack of them.

If they were lucky, they could knock out at least half of them before they reached the wall.

If they were lucky.

And luck was on their side, for when the actual forms of the attackers could be seen through the dust, many of

the horses were riderless. If they hadn't shot h... at least made a good-sized dent in the attackers... The townsmen kept up firing, kept it up eve... what was left of the war party split—some going... the east, some dropping from their racing, la... ponies and taking up positions.

"Now!" Jason shouted, and every fourth man... down the nearest ladder and headed for a new posi... A third of them went to the east, the rest to the sou...

Jason stayed right where he was, and he took... three warriors by the time it took his men to cross th... town square and mount the south wall.

Ward Wanamaker must have given Doc Morelli the... slip, because Jason thought he caught a glimpse of him, firing a handgun from the south wall. "Poor Apache didn't have a notion of what they were getting into," he muttered, momentarily cheered.

Then an arrow zinged into the throat of the man ne... to him, and he found himself holding the man ba... from falling from the scaffolding and urgently shou... for Doc Morelli.

Ward Wanamaker was still wobbly from Doc M... powders, but nobody was going to keep him from... ing today. It seemed to him that there were sur... fewer Apache out there, and he wondered why... they didn't just give up and go home. Their num... been seriously depleted, and he figured that it... an awfully long time before they had Apac... again in Fury.

least wounded by the whoop that the brave gave out before he twisted out of sight behind a clump of brush.

If nothing else, these Apache were surely brushing him up on his marksmanship, he thought. And then he missed one.

"Dad-blast it," he hissed, and took another shot. This one hit home and the brave fell forward, on his face.

Dr. Morelli came halfway up the ladder and called, "Anyone need me here?"

"Just keep down," Ward answered. "We're doin' all right for a bunch of sodbusters. How they doin' up north?"

"Two casualties, but no one killed. As of yet."

"I mean, how they doin' Indian-wise?"

"Jason says their ranks are much withered. He's expecting them to back off and go home at any moment."

Ward chuckled. "Well, me, too, but if wishes was horses . . ."

Doc Morelli showed a little smile and nodded. "I know. Frustrating, isn't it?"

Ward turned back toward the attacking Apache. And took a potshot at a brave a little too far off. His bullet had no effect, and he crouched down to reload.

"Take care of yourself, Ward," the doctor said.

"That's why I'm using my Colt. Don't make my shoulder hurt me near so bad."

"Good man," said the doctor, and slid down the ladder.

"I'm only good iffen I live through this," Ward muttered to himself as he chucked shell after shell into the handgun's chambers.

* * *

Jason signaled his men to hold their fire when he saw the braves trying to move east and take their wounded with them. He hoped and prayed that this was the sign he'd been waiting for—that they were giving up and going home. Finally.

One of the men, a wagon driver whose name Jason didn't know, kept on firing on the retreating Indians until Saul bashed him in the face with the butt of his rifle and broke his nose.

"Easy there, killer," Jason said.

"Oy, mein Gott," said Saul, sinking to his knees beside the fallen man.

"There wasn't anything else you could do," Jason said as he squeezed past, noting the trail of the last Apache warrior in sight.

The brave wasn't moving any too quickly. He was leading a pony upon which he'd balanced the body of his injured buddy.

The men had passed along his order to hold their fire, and not a shot rang out as Jason circled the town. "Keep your places, men," he said as he passed through them. "Just in case."

Although in truth, he had never seen a sorrier, more exhausted batch of men than those he crept around on his way to the south wall. Unless it was the Apache outside their walls.

And he knew exactly how they felt.

17

Megan MacDonald struggled awake, although she felt she was swimming, not waking.

She moved up, upward toward some dim, dim light she more felt than saw, upward until the light took on body, took on color, took on shape and then noise, and then, for no reason, clarity.

Her neck hurt.

She tried to raise her hand to it, but it wouldn't budge. She tried to speak, but her lips wouldn't move. She listened for the sounds of battle, but they, too, were absent.

And then she felt her lips flutter.

"Jenny?" she heard herself whisper. "J-Jenny?"

Dr. Morelli leaned into view. He smiled. "Back with us, I see!"

"W-what happened?" she managed. "Where am I?"

"It's all right," he said, and patted her hand, stroked her arm. "You're going to be fine. You're in our little makeshift hospital."

She winced and twisted her head slightly, and he added, "You were shot in the neck, Megan. Don't worry, I got the arrowhead out and stitched you up. You're a very lucky girl. An eighth of an inch to the side and . . . Well, all you'll have to show for your misadventure will be a tiny scar. I promise."

She must have visibly relaxed, because he smiled again. "Now, don't try to talk, don't try to do anything but sleep. Your friend, Jenny, has been sitting up with you all night. I just forced her to go get herself some breakfast."

She blinked, long and slow.

"That's the girl." He held a large spoon to her lips and said, "Now, take this. That's right. Just a little at a time . . . Good girl, Megan. Jason will be down to check on you in a bit. And yes," the doctor added, "he's fine. The Apache have backed off for the time being. Ward Wanamaker thinks we've got them beat."

Megan felt her lips curl up into a smile, which the doctor returned. "Close your eyes now, Megan. Rest."

She allowed herself to flutter her eyes closed, and just like that, she was asleep.

When Jason reached the southern wall of the stockade, there was not an Apache in sight. The only thing remaining of them was a dejected dust cloud, trailing slowly off toward the southeast.

He stood there staring at the retreating dust for what seemed like a long time, but was probably only a few minutes.

They were saved. The Apache were going away at

long last. Outside of a couple of razed ranches—and more than a few dead and wounded—the town had won.

And then slowly, as if someone were letting all the air out of him, he sank to his knees, then his seat, and passed out.

Saul Cohen was watching from across the way, and when he saw Jason begin the slow slide down to the planks upon which he'd been standing, he climbed down his ladder at the north wall and began to run across the square.

The only thing he could think was that Jason had been shot, although he couldn't see any blood.

But when he reached the other side of the town and scrambled up the nearest ladder, Jason wasn't shot with an arrow or stabbed by a spear. He was, very simply, unconscious.

Things were never that simple for Saul, though. He raised Jason's head and slapped him across the face as hard as he could. Jason's eyes immediately fluttered.

"Ouch!" he said, and rubbed at his cheek.

"Are you all right?" Saul demanded.

"Somebody just hit me," was Jason's groggy reply. "I think . . ."

Saul helped him to his feet. "Come down off this scaffolding, boy," he said. "If you cave in again, you won't have so far to fall."

"Wait a minute," Jason muttered, waving him off. He hauled himself up to peek between the spikes at the top of the stockade again, as if he needed to remind himself.

He'd been right. The Indians were in retreat. Even the bodies of their dead had been picked up and carried off.

He gave out with a huge sigh and let Saul help him down to the ground. "They're gone," he said. "They're really gone. For good this time, I think, Saul."

"May it please the Lord that you're right, Jason," Saul said, and tucked him under one arm—a difficult task since Jason was over six feet and Saul was only five-ten. With his boots on.

Slowly, they made their way up the alley and around the corner, to the livery and Dr. Morelli's makeshift hospital.

"Nothing but simple exhaustion," Morelli said, once they'd found Jason a cot and Morelli had taken a good look at him. "Although in this case, I think simple is too elementary a word."

Saul looked up from Jason's face in horror. "What? There's something else wrong?"

Morelli shook his head. "No, I just mean that this poor lad feels the weight of the world—at least our corner of it—on his shoulders. He's far too young to be saddled with such a heavy load."

Saul's brows twisted quizzically, and he asked, "So we should fire him? After he has saved us all once again?"

Morelli gave a chuckle. "No, Saul, no. The load may be heavy on Jason, but face it—he's the only man in town with the patience and upbringing to be our sheriff. His father was a great man, and the sapling doesn't sprout far from the tree," he added.

"Without Jason," he went on, "we would have all died back in Indian Territory at the hands of Quanah Parker."

"Without my dice, too," Saul added softly. The story of Saul's sugar cubes, made into dice so that they could gamble with the Indians for the captive girls, was fast turning into Cohen family legend.

"Yes, we can't forget your sugar-cube dice," Morelli said. Saul was surprised—and a little embarrassed—that Morelli had heard his mutter. Apparently, someone outside his family had remembered the incident, too. And also had excellent hearing. . . .

"Will he be all right?" he asked, wanting as much to change the subject as to find out about Jason.

Morelli nodded. "Yes, I'm sure he will. He just needs a good rest, that's all, with nothing preying on his mind."

Saul sighed heavily. "Thank the Good Lord."

"Yes, indeed. And our brave townspeople, too."

Saul nodded. *Well, some of them,* he thought.

Lone Wolf dropped out of the sad caravan of beaten Apache, leaving Clever Eyes to lead them the rest of the way home.

Not him, though. He would not go back in shame. He would not dishonor his father and his wives and sons with his ineptitude. He would not hear his name mingled with laughter around the campfires, nor would he wish to hear it in sadness or anger each time a fallen brave was mentioned.

And there were many to mention. Far too many.

He was going back to the town that white men called Fury.

He would find the one in charge, and he would fight him, hand to hand.

He would be victorious and return to the home fires vindicated.

Or, at the least, with some of his shame lifted.

Moving on foot, Curly, Carlos, and Wilmer made their way from what was left of the MacDonald ranch and toward town.

Carlos had drawn them all plenty of water from the well, so they didn't suffer from thirst, although they did suffer from the burden of carrying it. Wilmer had found several overlooked sheepskins hanging on the far fence, and he'd gone through them and found the three best, the three that he could make fairly watertight.

He'd done a good job. Water dripped from all three hide bags, but at least none had let loose a gushing flood as yet.

But they were heavy. Especially when you were trying to walk almost ten miles through the heat of an Arizona spring.

But then, ten miles might be just the start, Curly thought. When they got to Fury, there might not be any Fury left. All that smoke had to come from something. Like a town burning to the ground.

The Apache probably only stayed today to polish off the survivors.

He wanted to weep, to throw himself down on the sand like a girl and just cry and cry.

But he didn't. He, along with the other two men, just

kept on trudging and sweating and praying that he wouldn't find what he expected.

At long last, the Reverend Milcher allowed his family to climb up out of the Indian shelter he had dug under the altar. His wife, Lavinia, took a deep breath as she climbed up the ladder. He didn't blame her. Below, everything stank of raw earth and the grave. Up here, however, everything stank of burned wood and scorched fabric.

But the sounds of the church were what interested him most. Not the sounds of the church itself so much, but the lack of sound from outside.

It was still light, but there were no gunshots, no shouting, no sounds of arrows thudding into their hapless targets. There was only the sound of everyday activity. Of men calling everyday comments to one another, of women calling to their children.

Without realizing it, he relaxed. They had survived, with God's help. He closed his eyes and gave thanks to his Father in Heaven.

There must be wounded that he could minister to, those injured who would take succor in the comforting word of the Lord.

Gesturing to Lavinia to keep the children inside, he walked outside and down the street, toward Dr. Morelli's house. But he didn't have to go that far. On his way, he came across all the wounded in the livery.

Someone had set up rows of makeshift cots, two or three to a stall and end to end down the aisle. Or at least, what was left of the aisle. Fire had taken a toll on the livery as it had on his house and church. Half the livery's roof was caved in and the hay in the loft was gone, as was part of the interior of the stable itself.

Someone had taken the initiative to clear it up, though. Rubble was piled out in the street, and animals were stabled in the best of the burned but intact stalls with nothing but sky overhead for protection from the elements.

He finally found Dr. Morelli and pulled him aside. "Might I be of some help, Doctor?" He clutched his Bible near his heart and pushed back his shoulders. He must let these last few days pass from his mind. He was a man of God, and he would look the part.

Morelli stared at him. "I trust you mean more of a help than you've been these last few days?"

Milcher stiffened. "Excuse me?"

"You've been conspicuously absent, Reverend. There are some here who would have welcomed a visit from you or your wife."

Despite himself, Milcher felt his cheeks color hotly. "I'm sorry," he said. "I have been caring for my own family, seeing that no harm came to them, and constantly engaged in prayer for our population's deliverance."

Morelli picked up a damp rag and began to scrub at his fingers. "And I'm sure that everybody's grateful. Just as grateful as I am."

Milcher wasn't certain whether or not he was being made sport of. So he said, "May I start at the far end and work my way up?"

"Whatever you want," Morelli said, his attention on

his fingernails and the cloth. "Just don't wake up anybody who's asleep."

Milcher nodded.

"Or dead," Morelli added.

Milcher wanted to make a subtly cutting remark, but Morelli had turned away and moved to the next patient.

So instead, grumbling beneath his breath, he slowly walked to the far end of the livery and entered the last stall.

"Good afternoon," he said to the men on the cots inside. "May I share the word of our Lord with you?"

The wagon train

They weren't far out of Fury now.

In fact, Blake was certain they'd make it tomorrow. They hadn't seen any more smoke rising, but he thought he'd heard the faint sound of distant gunfire. It could just be his ears tricking him, he thought. Sadly, his hearing hadn't been the same since the war.

His captain should have had to spend a few weeks standing next to that cannon, he thought, then immediately reprimanded himself. War was a thankless job, and everyone had to serve where they were needed. Even if it meant they'd go partially deaf in one ear. It was a small price to pay considering what other men had given up: their arms, their legs, their lives.

To take his mind off his physical worries, he began to think about Fury, and the townspeople that would likely greet them there. From Arlo Baxter, the man he'd talked to about the little town, he'd learned that it had been named for the famous wagon master, Jedediah

Fury, who had led them from Kansas City and later perished in the Indian Territory. Comanche, he thought the man had said. Such a shame. The man had been a true legend.

But the wagon master's son had brought them the rest of the way, and was now the town sheriff. That was nice. It was rather circular actually.

There were many shops there at which a small wagon train could restock, if they planned to go on to California, and a doctor to see to your aches and pains if you had any. He'd like the doctor to have a look at little Seth, just because.

Seth had been born without a doctor present, and had yet to avail himself of a medical man. The baby showed no signs of anything wrong, let alone out of the ordinary, but still, the Reverend Blake liked to stay on the safe side.

He might ask the doctor to check out Laura, too.

Just to be on the safe side.

He wanted Olin to have his wagon checked over as well, and perhaps acquire a new spare axle. If it hadn't been for the first spare axle, well, Blake didn't like to think of the pickle they'd have found themselves in.

He was thinking that maybe he and Laura and Seth would just stay on in Fury, but had no idea what the others planned. Although he imagined they'd go on. He knew that Olin was set on California and the sea, and that Mankiller was set on mining for gold or silver.

Mining was good in Arizona, or so he'd been told, but for gold, Blake supposed the Mankillers would need to go to California, up toward Sutter's Mill. If it hadn't already been mined dry.

He shrugged. His business was God, not gold.

The day was clear and not overly hot, wildflowers spread before them like an endless pink and yellow and lavender quilt, and things were going well.

Why borrow trouble?

18

Jason tossed and turned in his bed.

Dr. Morelli had given him enough sleeping powder to quiet a grizzly, but Jason was too torn up emotionally to be quieted by anything short of a .44 to the brain.

Fearing to give him any more powders, Morelli watched helplessly. Helpless should be his middle name, Morelli thought. Jason was getting a sleepless sleep, the Reverend Milcher was loose and spouting God-knows-what rhetoric among his patients, and if anyone should be taking a dose of his sleeping powder, it should be Morelli himself.

Night would be falling soon. He hoped his patients would sleep through till dawn, for then perhaps he could do the same. That's what he wanted at this stage, wanted it more than anything. He wanted it for Olympia, too. She'd been awake nearly as long as he, and she'd been hard at work making the food to fuel them.

Yet he wished the same for the town's sheriff and his deputy. Jason—and to a lesser extent Ward—had been going at it day and night, and Ward was twice wounded.

Jason had only taken a flesh wound, but it had knocked him down completely. A man needed to sleep, didn't he?

It was an impossible circumstance, any way you looked at it.

He heard the Reverend Milcher's voice droning in the background: "And yea, though I walk through the valley of the shadow of death, I will fear no evil, for Thou art with me. . . ."

As much as he disliked Milcher, Morelli hoped, for once, that he was right.

Hoped it with all his heart.

Lone Wolf stopped when the shadows grew long, and made camp within a small stand of palo verde trees. He would sleep well tonight, for he wished to be well rested for the coming battle with the chief of the whites.

After he ate his supper—a hare he had killed along the ride north—he whetted his knife on the sharpening stone he carried, polishing it to a fine, surgical edge. He would be victorious tomorrow, there could be no question of it.

But to be on the safe side, he offered up prayers, offered them in chanting and in smoke.

He was asleep by ten thirty, and dreamed of slicing the white leader's throat, dreamed of the blood gushing out, and dreamed of his people at their fires, proud.

Saul Cohen made his pallet on the floor, alongside his boys. Rachael had fallen asleep hours ago, and he had played cards—Go Fish and Old Maid mainly—with the boys until one by one they had fallen asleep.

A fine thing this is, he'd thought while he made them comfortable and tucked them in. *That a boy's last memory of his papa should be a game of Old Maid.*

Now, Jason had said that the Apache had folded their blankets and gone home, but then, he'd said that before. And he'd been wrong before. Why should this time be any different?

Of course, Jason had been right many more times than he had been wrong, but this little statistic slipped Saul's mind for the moment. All he wanted was his Rachael and his boys and a safe place to live.

A nice place to live.

This had been the nicest place he had lived in a very long time. Maybe ever. Only a few people in town despised them—Reverend Milcher and a few of his cronies—but no one had tried to set fire to their house—except the Apache, who hated everybody, it seemed—and no one had tried to run them out of town. Or burn their house. Or kill their livestock. Or poison their well.

If those blasted Indians would leave them alone, Saul was convinced that he and Rachael could live here forever and watch the town grow up around them. And he believed that had Rachael been awake, she would have agreed with him. Hadn't she already begun sorting out the dishes and silver to make a second kitchen in the house? Hadn't she already purchased a new boiler and baking sheets and set them aside? Was this something that a woman who was thinking of moving on would do?

Yes, his Rachael wanted to stay, too. He sighed and

smiled before his thoughts returned to his friend Jason and those blasted Apache.

He hoped Jason was right. He hoped the Apache were gone for good and all.

Curly, Carlos, and Wilmer had stopped about an hour back. They were only a little over a mile out of town, but Curly didn't believe he was up to looking at what was left of it this evening.

It could wait until tomorrow.

He stretched out on his blanket. The whole bloody mess could wait until tomorrow, so far as he was concerned. He'd seen what horrible things an Apache could do to a white man, and he was not looking forward to seeing what had happened to the people in town.

Next to him, Wilmer stood, ringing what would be his sleeping place with a rope.

"What are you doin', Wilmer?" Curly asked, although he already knew.

Wilmer explained that he was keeping rattlesnakes from climbing into his bedroll with him. Now, Curly had heard this old wives' tale more times than he could count—about how the rattler thought it was another snake that he was trying to climb over, and took off for fear of being bitten. Curly had to admit he'd seen it work. Once. And that rattler must have been dumber than a post if he thought that prickly old chunk of dead hemp was another snake.

Besides, they climbed over each other all the time, didn't they?

But he didn't want to get started with Wilmer—or

with Carlos, who'd already ringed his pallet and was fast asleep.

"Ain't you afeared of snakes?" Wilmer asked, startling him.

"What?"

"I said, ain't you afeared of snakes," Wilmer replied a little testily. "I got enough rope to do us both."

Curly started to launch into his reasons *not* to do it, but decided he didn't have the strength, particularly in the case of a stubborn pudding-head like Wilmer.

"Fine, Wilmer," he sighed, and rolled over so at least he didn't have to see the skinny idiot spread the stupid loop around him. Through clenched teeth, he added, "That'd be right nice of you."

Wilmer spread the loop.

Jason did indeed sleep through the night, and when he woke with the dawn he actually felt . . . good! He checked on a still-sleeping Megan and found her doing well—or at least Jenny and Doc Morelli said so. She looked to be of better color than the day before, though, and he was encouraged.

When he walked out of the livery and onto the town square, Saul Cohen, already awake and on the wall, informed him that there were no Apache in sight.

Next he went back in the livery to check on Ward, who was sawing logs like mad. Rather than disturb him, Jason hied himself over to the house.

He didn't enter, but went directly to the stable, where he grained his mare and Jenny's and their father's old roan horse and fed the chickens, then turned the horses out into the corral with the Mortons' draft stock and mucked out the stalls.

The garden needed a good watering, but he put that off until later. Next, he had to go turn his prisoner loose.

When he got to the jail, he found Matt MacDonald up and awake, and talking to one of his hands, Curly Lohan, through the bars of his cell.

"Everything?" Matt was asking when Jason walked in.

"Morning, gents," Jason said. "And congratulations to you," he said to Curly.

"What?" said Curly.

"For making it back to town! When we saw your smoke, we figured you were as good as dead. Other boys make it out okay, too?"

Curly seemed a little surprised, but he said, "Yeah, they did. We was pretty surprised to find the town still here, too. Seen the smoke. Thought you was goners. Glad to see we was wrong," he added, grinning, and stuck out his hand.

Jason shook it. "Thanks, Curly. We're pretty happy about it, too."

Curly just kept shaking his hand, and Jason finally had to pull away. He covered by immediately fetching the key and unlocking Matt's cell. "Time to let this monkey out," he said.

Matt grumbled, "I'll monkey you, Mr. Tin Badge. . . ."

"Best hold those comments for folks with lesser hearing, MacDonald," Jason said. He put the key away. He'd be glad to get rid of Matt and have his office all to himself again. "How'd you get out of being burned, Curly?"

"We stayed down in those hidey-holes Mr. MacDonald—I mean, that Gil Whatshisname feller—had dug under the bunkhouse when he was workin' for the spread and they was puttin' up the buildings. The house, too."

"Gil Collins, you mean?" Jason asked, but he slid Matt an accusing look.

Curly said, "Yessir, that's him."

"Fella keeps getting himself almost killed," said Jason.

"Huh?"

"Ask your boss," Jason said. It had been because of Matt that Gil had got himself stove up the first time two years back. Even Morelli had taken a look at him and pronounced him dead. That is, until he sat up in his coffin the next afternoon and asked for water, beefsteak, and the doctor, in that order.

This time it had been because he hadn't seen the Indian on the gate.

But he was getting better, too. Jason had checked. He was beginning to think of him as Gil *O'*Collins, seeing as how he seemed to have the luck of the Irish.

"Will you move your damn feet?" Matt barked. His hands were pushing at the cell door.

Curly jumped back, and the cell door hit him in the face. "Ouch," he said, rubbing his wounded eyebrow.

"You best go over to the livery and see Doc Morelli," Jason said.

"Stop telling my man what to do!" shouted Matt. "Now, where's your sister, Fury?"

"Believe she's across the way, at the livery. Seeing to *your* sister."

"What's wrong with Megan?"

"Took an arrow in the neck." When Matt looked stricken, Jason added, "Don't worry, she's all right. She's got the best care in the world. Jenny was with her when it happened and got her to Morelli right away."

Matt's face visibly relaxed, and suddenly Jason wished he'd strung out the information a little more. Damn Matt anyway!

Jason sat down across the room, behind his desk. "Go on, Matt. Get the hell out of here."

Matt slammed the door behind him, leaving Curly in the office, blinking.

Jason smiled. "You can go, too, Curly."

"Th-thanks." Curly left the office, too, although Jason noted that he headed for Rollie Biggston's place. "Atta boy, Curly," Jason muttered.

Ward Wanamaker was awake and ambulatory, and had joined Saul Cohen up on the stockade. "Gettin' used to the place?" he asked as he sat down next to Saul. "Reckon you could bring some chintz up and make the place real homey, if you was of a mind to."

Saul chuckled. "Did Dr. Morelli kick you out?"

Ward shook his head. "Naw, it was the reverend. Couldn't stand it anymore."

"Milcher?"

"Only got but the one, last I heard."

Saul shook his head. "Sad but true, my friend. How is Miss Megan doing?"

"Pretty fair, I think. Jenny's still sittin' with her."

"She has a good heart, that one."

"Yeah, she sure enough does. You take a look out there lately?" Ward indicated the world beyond the stockade.

"No," said Saul halfheartedly.

Ward levered himself up carefully, watching both the stockade wall and the lip of the boards he was standing on. When he rose up to his full height, he looked out through the spikes at the top. He stared for a very long time, not moving.

"Ward?" asked Saul.

Nothing.

"Ward, what is it?"

"Come up here, Saul."

Saul gingerly stood up, too. When he peeked through the spikes, down to the land outside and below, he knew why Ward had frozen.

There, down below them and about forty feet out from the stockade wall, was a lone Apache warrior in full war paint, singing his death song: a thing that Saul, now that he had no more stockade logs blocking it, could hear clearly. And he was frightened.

"I'd best go get Jason," Ward said, and he was gone.

19

"Wait, wait, wait," Jason said, holding up his hands. "Start over!"

"You heard me the first time," Ward growled, and pulled Jason to his feet, using his good arm. "He wants the leader of the whites to come fight him, and he's serious. He's singin' his death song, in case you want t'know just how serious he is."

"Alone?"

"Yes, goddamn it!"

Jason blinked three times in rapid succession, as if waking from a deep sleep, and then he straightened. "What weapons?"

"Knives."

"Aw, crud."

"Don't worry, I set the freighter's smithy to whetting you the finest blade he could lay his hands on."

Jason sniffed. He had never been very good with a knife. "That's comforting." He walked forward and opened the door, ushering Ward out before him. "When's this supposed to happen?"

"Whenever you show up, I guess. Though he did say something about high noon."

"Good. I like noontime," Jason said facetiously. "Sun doesn't get in your eyes unless you look straight up. Just burns the living crud out of you."

"Could be worse," said Ward. "Could be July."

The two men walked purposefully across the square, behind the livery, and up the nearest ladder. Jason could hear the death song now, just faintly. It was tuneless, as far as he could figure, and that brave had no business singing it—or any other song. Or tune.

Or collection of random things that were supposed to be notes.

Jason listened for a moment to what he considered to be just noise. "What's he saying?" he asked Ward.

Ward shrugged. "More death song."

"This fight he wants to have. Is it supposed to be to the death then? Or is he doing it just to scare us?"

"He's an Apache. Is there any other kind than the first?"

"Figures."

Jason sighed. Just when you thought things were over, they weren't.

"He ain't got no more braves with him. Only thing he brought was that red and white pony, tied out to the left, back behind those prickly pears." Ward gestured, stabbing his finger until Jason saw the pinto tethered behind the cactus.

"What happens if he wins?"

"He goes home and they have a big party. And he probably saves a little face."

"And then he comes back to polish off the rest of us?"

Ward thought about it for a second before he said, "I reckon so."

"And if I win?"

"Then I don't reckon he goes home at all."

"Retribution?"

Ward shrugged.

Jason didn't have a good feeling about this, but before he could say anything, Saul Cohen, who he'd forgotten was there behind him, said, "I'll go in your place, Jason. They don't know your face."

Jason wheeled about. There was not one flicker of fear or even apprehension on Saul's face. How the heck did he do that?

Slowly, Jason shook his head. "God bless you, Saul, but no. You have a wife and children who need you, and who'd never forgive me if I got you killed on my account. But there is something you can do."

"Anything."

"I want Ward to come along and translate." Next to him, Ward nodded.

Jason turned back toward Saul. "And I need you to stay up here. If the Apache takes me down, I want you to kill him before he can make it to that pony and ride back to his people."

Saul started to open his mouth, but before he could utter a peep, Jason added, "If you have to pretend that he's going to turn any moment and shoot at you, then pretend."

A hint of a smile ticked at the edges of Saul's lips. "Yes, Jason. I'll do it."

Jason clapped him on the shoulder. "Knew you would, buddy." Then to Ward, he said, "C'mon. I've got our best man to back me up."

"But goldang it, Jason!" Ward kept grumbling as they made their way into the livery. "Why you got to fight him anyway? It ain't like the whole Apache nation's out there watchin', and gonna give you a turkey iffen you win and the promise to leave you on your own for the rest'a your natural life."

"I know that, Ward." He climbed through a broken window, and Ward followed.

"But Jason . . . Oh, cripes! I just don't get you at all sometimes. And why do we gotta go through the window all the time?"

"That's all right, Ward," he replied. "The window was closer. And I don't get me either."

Jason found Jenny, who reacted slightly more violently than had Ward.

In fact, she wept and beat on Jason's chest with her fists. And then she cursed him up one side and down the other for being six kinds of a fool.

And then she asked the same question that Ward had. "Why don't you just go back up there and shoot him? They attacked us, not the other way round. They don't have any sense of fairness or decency. Why should you show them any at all?"

He looked at her for a moment before he said, "Somebody's got to do to the right thing, Jenny."

"But why's it always *us*?" she called after him. "Why is it always *you*?"

Ward was wondering the same thing, but he didn't give his questions voice. He just did what he always did—said, "Yes, Jason," or "No, Jason," and did what he was told. And hated himself for it sometimes.

"It's comin' on noon," he said softly.

"I know," Jason replied. They'd made the rounds and told everybody of importance what Jason planned to do—and to hold their fire. They were almost back around to the south gate again.

"You ready?" Jason said when they reached it.

"Ready as I'll ever be," Ward said, wishing he were back East, cleaning out somebody's outhouse. Anything but this.

Jason unstrapped his six-gun and hung it on a post. "That better be there when I get back," he told Salmon Kendall. They had collected quite a group of followers on their way around the town, and Mayor Kendall was right up front.

Kendall slid it off the post and onto his arm. "I'd admire to hold on to it for you, Jason," he said.

"And Ward's, too," Jason said, motioning to Ward to take off his gun, too.

Ward hesitated a little too long—it was against his religion to go anywhere near a wild Indian without a weapon at his side, if not in hand—but at last he sighed and stripped himself of his gun belt.

Mayor Kendall accepted his rig, too.

And Ward figured that the next time they had an

election—here or anyplace else—he was going to run for mayor, not deputy.

And he was *definitely* not going to toss his hat into the ring for sheriff!

Jason took the big Arkansas toothpick into his hand and gently ran it over his arm. It left behind a thin red line that dripped blood. "Nice," he said with a smile to the man who'd whetted it.

The man smiled back. "We aim to please," he replied. And he was the first of them to say, "Best of luck to you, Sheriff."

Jason nodded while Ward and the others chimed in with their felicitations as well, although Ward noticed that nobody wished him luck. Nobody ever wished the deputy luck, dad-blast it.

Somebody opened the gate's latch, and it swung in toward them.

The crowd quieted.

"All right, Ward. Let's do it." Jason stepped into the opening and out the gate, and into the stark rays of the noontime sun.

Against his better intuition, Ward followed along behind.

"Close it up, men," Jason shouted, and blast them if they didn't do it without so much as a by-your-leave!

Ward felt a distinct whistle of cowardly wind flicker over his backside as the gate slammed closed and the latch went back down with a dull and very final thud.

The Apache, who had been sitting on the ground and silent when they first stepped out, rose to his feet. He was tall for an Apache. Ward guessed him at about six

Olin did, and made out a few figures. With a little adjusting of the lenses, he discovered two white men facing an Indian. One of the white men was standing well back from the other two men, and what Olin could see of the lip of the southern wall of the town was lined with men, like spectators at a prize fight.

"What the hell?" he muttered.

"Exactly," said Blake. "I think we need to wait and see what happens before we go trotting in there big as life. Don't you?"

Slowly, Olin nodded.

The white man was wounded, Lone Wolf noted as he walked nearer. His shoulder was bandaged.

Good. A weak point, right from the start.

This would be his day, this would be an Apache day. He would gut this pale one with no trouble.

Jason had started his march toward the brave slowly, as he moved nearer, his steps grew in confidence, lly longer, decidedly firmer.

had several things in his favor, he figured. First, es usually didn't sharpen their blades on both His was, and both sides were like razors. No ow he struck the man, his blade would slice.

d, he'd had training, thanks to the U.S. Army, in and fighting. All right, that didn't count for n it came to outwitting an Apache, but he'd

feet. And he was as lean and muscular as Jason was, maybe leaner and more muscular.

Great.

Ward found himself wishing that he'd kept that little pocket gun he'd taken off Rollie Biggston last year. He had a feeling it would come in awful handy in a minute or two.

"Tell him who we are and ask what he wants," Jason said.

"Like we don't know," Ward muttered before he spoke up in Apache. "This is Jason Fury, the high sheriff of our city. I am only an interpreter. Jason Fury comes armed as you said, and only, as you said, with one blade. He says he will fight you now, but not until he knows your name."

Ward translated what he'd said for Jason, then listened while the Indian spoke. He translated this, too: "I am called Lone Wolf. I carry one blade, as I have told you, and nothing more."

Jason said, "Thanks, Ward. You ask him, if I win this fight, are his people gonna leave us alone?"

Ward jabbered, then the Apache jabbered, then Ward said, "Yup."

"That took you long enough," Jason grumbled. "You sure you didn't recite the Gettysburg Address in there somewhere?"

Ward just looked at him.

Jason said, "Well, how long are they gonna leave us alone for?"

"Didn't say."

"But—"

"I wouldn't press him on it, Jason."

"Aw, crud . . . Well, I suppose we'd best get to fighting."

Ward repeated Jason's comments to Lone Wolf—except for the "Aw, crud" part—and Lone Wolf replied to him at length.

"He says to take your shirt off," Ward told Jason.

"Why?" Jason knew he'd bake bright red in no time at all.

"You're lucky he didn't tell you to strip outta them pants, too," Ward said, and Jason finally took him at his word.

He shucked out of the sleeves of his flannel shirt, then tossed it over to Ward.

"Just as well," he said. "Keep it from gettin' all full of holes like the last one."

He stood up a little straighter, the knife in his right hand, its blade pointed up and out. "Tell him c'mon, let's go."

20

The wagon train

Olin Whaler nearly ran his rig into the back of Blake's, for Blake called a halt and Laura, startled, had reined their team in very suddenly.

Olin jumped down from the seat and stormed f___ ward. "What's wrong with you, man?" he demand__ Blake. "Somebody could'a been killed! And__ almost to Fury," he added, pointing toward the___ the distance. Actually, it looked more like a ___ being lined all around with a tall stockade f___

Blake got down off his horse and unslu___ ulars from around his neck. He hande___ with a curt, "Take a look."

Olin held them up to his eyes. Th___ ade walls of the town, which he ___ chopped into points at the top. Th___ the base of the wall nearest hi___ afire, then put out before mu___

"What am I supposed to be___

"Look to the south," replied ___

been involved in a skirmish or two since coming West, and he thought he could figure out the brave's moves.

He hoped he could, that is.

And lastly, he had Saul up on the stockade.

If he was killed—a thing he was fervently trusting wouldn't happen—then Saul would blast the brave so at least he couldn't go home and brag about his victory to the other war chiefs.

One way or the other, Jason figured that the town of Fury was saved. And that had been the goal all along, hadn't it?

Well, that, and to keep on living and to marry Megan MacDonald and to see somebody nice matched up with his sister, Jenny, and . . . He stopped walking. The brave stopped, too, a few feet from him.

The brave said something Jason didn't understand. But Jason said, "Same to you, friend."

The brave tossed his knife from hand to hand. Jason did not. He was afraid he'd drop it. He simply scowled and took a wider stance.

With no warning, the brave leaped toward him, blade first. Jason leaped to the side, narrowly missing the brave's outstretched blade while he lashed out with his own in midair. He felt the knife meet something, but could tell it hadn't gone deep.

He landed on his feet, automatically spinning around and crouching just in time to brace for a second attack.

This time he jumped back while nicking a narrow slice down the brave's heavily muscled back. He thought it was a clean cut, but when the brave turned around, Jason glimpsed a thin, bloody length of skin limply flapping.

The brave had yet to wound him, let alone touch him. *Don't get cocky,* he told himself.

But it came too late. The brave screamed, scaring Jason half to death, and charged again. This time, he felt the knife rapidly whittling at his bandage, felt the sunlight strike what had been tender, pampered flesh, felt a new gush of blood.

Atop the stockade, Saul gasped and clutched his rifle tighter.

No, no, no, Jason! he thought he screamed, but it was all inside his head. For a moment he thought he'd squeezed the trigger, too, but the sight was still firm to his eye, and the rifle's trigger waited beneath his finger.

There was blood, so much blood. . . .

Jason didn't know whether the old wound had just opened up, or the Apache had created a new one. He only knew that he had to put a stop to this before it went any further.

The two men, each maddened by impatience, began to wildly attack each other: no planning, no thought, no rules. They fought like wild animals, desperate creatures, and less than half the time when Jason lashed out did he meet more than air.

The Apache wasn't having any more luck striking Jason's body. Although Jason felt the knife slice into his arm, across his belly, and skitter along his ribs, the misses by the brave far outnumbered the hits, and all

Jason's wounds were shallow. More times than not, he was able to block a thrust before the Apache's blade could penetrate flesh.

It was just that they were both moving so fast, so desperately.

And at last, Jason once again came into himself and actually began to think. This time it was he who snatched the second it took to form a shaky plan.

Simultaneously, he shrieked and attacked, and it was the Apache warrior who momentarily froze in shock.

Jason charged, but didn't swerve. And as he was sinking his blade directly into the savage's chest, just as he was thinking that this was far too easy—and what had he been so nervous about anyway?—Jason felt his opponent's knife plunge deep into his shoulder.

Skewered on the blade of the white called Jason Fury, Lone Wolf did the only thing he could—he thrust his knife hard into his opponent's shoulder. He hoped he had found the joint.

This white might kill him, but at least he would maim him, Lone Wolf thought. At least he might steal the use of his arm from him.

The white's knife was dancing dangerously close to his heart, and he felt the hooves of death pounding, galloping nearer and nearer. But he would not go willingly to be with his ancestors.

With his last strength, he twisted his blade.

* * *

The two struggled for a moment, closer than dancers, each one grimacing in pain and frustration, their screams of agony just skimming over the surface of expression. And the cheering, hooting crowd on the stockade wall went swiftly silent.

The blade in his shoulder pinned his arm, grated against his joint, but Jason threw everything he had into his knife hand, forcing it up and just slightly to the side.

But just slightly was all it took.

Suddenly, fluid gushed from the man's chest wound and his opponent went limp in his arms. Jason let him slide to the ground, and when he backed away from the crumpled corpse—Lone Wolf's chest was bathed in blood from that one last, frantic gush—Jason sat down, hard, and fell back in a dead faint.

And his last thought, before he passed out and dropped into a deep well of soft, welcoming black, was pleasure that now Saul wouldn't have to shoot somebody that wasn't shooting back at him.

"Hello the gate!" Blake called. He had put on his collar at Laura's insistence, and sat his horse ramrod straight. "Hello, somebody!"

Faintly, he heard a male voice call, "Open the gate, somebody. Visitors!"

Blake allowed himself a sigh of relief. There was someone in there alive after all.

Then the gate swung open, and the four wagons of his little train passed through the gate while Blake stayed outside, watching over them. When they were safely inside, he rode in after them and the gate was closed behind him.

A man came up to him and grabbed his horse's reins. But the man seemed friendly—at least he was smiling—so Blake took no offense.

"Howdy!" said the man, and introduced himself as Ward Wanamaker, the town's deputy sheriff. Blake wondered where the sheriff was, but said nothing.

"Glad to see you folks," Deputy Wanamaker went on. "Glad you came when you did. If you'd come a day earlier, you would'a likely ended up dead. We been havin' some Indian trouble, which is why the town's locked up tighter than a tick."

"I see," said Blake, not correcting the deputy's simile while thanking the Good Lord for their broken axle. "We thought we saw smoke a couple of days past. Was that part of your trouble?"

"Yup, sure was," said Wanamaker. "Long story. Which I'd be glad to tell you over a beer." His eyes flicked to Blake's collar. "That is, if it ain't against your religion, Reverend."

Blake shook his head. The promise of a real beer was music to his ears, and already had his mouth watering. "I'd like to get my people settled first, but yes, that sounds wonderful. Where should I meet you?"

The deputy jabbed a thumb over his shoulder. "Right here, at Biggston's," he said. "But I'll come along and get you settled in. 'Fraid you'll have to stay in your wagons for the time being. We're fresh out of anyplace to put you up."

As he rode after the wagons and the deputy strolled at his side, Blake looked around at the town, saw the burned-out buildings, and also saw the people, joyous at their deliverance. He made up his mind. This was the place they'd stay and put down roots.

This was home.

"Jason?" Saul Cohen's voice.

"Oh, Jason, please wake up," he heard Jenny weep.

"Now, I've told you folks. It's sheer exhaustion more than any wound." Now, the soothing tones from Dr. Morelli washed over him. Jenny said he had a good "bedside manner," and she was right. "If you'll all back off and let him sleep, he'll be right as rain when he wakes up. Aside from that shoulder wound, that is."

Jason tried to reach to feel his shoulder, but could no more move his hand than open his mouth. He felt himself sinking down again into the blackness, a sinking that came from inside and felt so calming, so good. *Is this what dying is like?*

Mayor Kendall's voice came next. "Well, exactly how long do you feel this might take, Morelli?"

Jason heard the sounds of people being herded out the door, heard their protests turning to mutters with distance, and then he heard a door quietly close.

The inner darkness enveloped him again.

Megan was getting better each day, but not enough that Morelli would let her get up from her cot as yet. Jenny sat beside her, going on and on about Jason, and what he had done for the town, and what a wonderful brother he was, and so on and so forth.

And Megan could listen as long as Jenny wanted to go on. As angry as she'd been with Jason on the day she rode into town—how long ago had that been?—she was filled with love for him now.

Love for him because he'd arrested her brother rather than let him ride, hell-bent for leather and full of pride, straight into a swarm of Apache; because Jenny was going to stay here with him, in town, and she loved Jenny almost as much as she loved Jason; and because he'd done the impossible—he'd saved the town of Fury, lock, stock, and barrel.

Saved it—and them all—once again.

Now, these were but a few of the things Jenny had told her while she lay here, unable to reply or even open her eyes. She'd heard Curly come through, too, with the news that their house was burned to the ground and all the outbuildings, too, but that he and Carlos and Wilmer were all right, though the blasted Apache had made off with their horses. She was sorry for their captured mounts, who were likely being whipped silly—if not served up for dinner—by their new owners, but otherwise overjoyed for the three hands' good fortune.

She hoped that her wound wouldn't be hideous when it healed. She hoped it wouldn't show at all. She couldn't imagine Jason paired with anyone less than perfect—not even her!

She pictured him in her mind—his blond hair bleached almost white by the Arizona sun, his once-pale skin bronzed by the same culprit, and those pale, blue, mesmerizing eyes, those eyes you could fall into, and fall and fall and fall. . . .

She sighed, and heard Jenny cry, "Doctor! Oh, Dr. Morelli, come quick!" Although she couldn't see it, she heard the happiness in Jenny's voice. "Megan smiled!"

The newcomers had been settled in, and now Ward Wanamaker strolled down to Jason's house, feeling as full of himself as if it had been he who had killed that Apache brave with his own two hands. He rapped at the door. It felt funny to knock since he lived here most of the time, but in a few seconds, Susannah Morton answered the door.

Immediately, she smiled and asked him in. Over tea, he brought them up to date on the current situation. Susannah and her sister-in-law, Eliza, oohed and ahhed in all the right places, and Miss Electa and Miss Europa softly oh-myed or gasped when they weren't pouring tea or offering him more of the funny little sandwiches that Susannah had made.

When he finished everything he could think of to tell them, Miss Europa—whom he had never thought of as Mrs. Griggs, although he should have—asked when they might go home, seeing as how the Indians had gone south and according to him, were not expected back.

It left him in a bit of a muddle, since only the sheriff could give them permission, and the sheriff, Jason, was unconscious at the moment. They'd been bravely defended from the Apache menace by Ward himself, of course. But he told them they'd have to wait for Jason, and that was all there was to it.

All four women nodded, and that was the end of it.

But on his way out the front door, Miss Electa pulled him aside.

"Deputy Wanamaker," she began shyly, "thank you for taking the time from your busy schedule to keep us apprised of the town's matters. We are *most* sincerely grateful." She gave his arm a soft squeeze on the word "most."

Well, Ward couldn't make it back to the office fast enough. This was all wrong!

Jenny was the one he wanted, even though she was married to somebody else. He didn't want wizened Electa Morton. Why, she was old, probably as old as he was, for cripe's sake, and talked like a Kansas City banker to boot!

Just the thought of it shook him so badly that when he got back to the office, he drank half of the bottle of whiskey that he'd hidden in the bottom drawer of the file cabinet.

The wagons around the well in the center of town showed no signs of moving on, and not because their owners had been told to stay. The people were simply exhausted—and hungry.

Olympia Morelli had the cook fires going again, and was brewing up a kettle of stew the size of which was reported to be someplace between two nail kegs, stood end to end, and the size of a grand piano's sound box.

As usual, it was a good, thick stew: full of big chunks of beef and potatoes, with beans and corn and tomatoes and onions, and sided by Olympia's own excellent biscuits with sweet cream butter and wild mesquite honey. Or fruit preserves, for those with more exotic tastes.

All the men in town were either drunk or stuffing themselves with Olympia's bounty, or both.

The newcomers joined in the feast, too, and were more than happy to taste Olympia's cooking. One of the ladies was overheard to say that it was the best stew she'd ever tasted. Aside from her own, of course.

Almost all the womenfolk were keeping themselves busy cleaning. After all, they'd had smoke or dust blown into their homes for days, or tracked in by bleeding husbands or sons. And most of the time they hadn't been allowed to do anything about it. They'd stayed inside, hiding with the children as they'd been told to.

But even they got a bite or two of Olympia's stew.

Even Rollie Biggston, drunk as a skunk, waddled up the street to Olympia's outdoor kitchen. "Shtew!" he managed to belt out.

Jenny, who was manning the kettle while Olympia made the rounds of the shut-ins, grabbed a bowl, ladled in two dippers of the rich concoction, and stuck a spoon in it. "Shtew to you, too!" she said as she handed it to him.

"Thankth," he said, and waddled away, leaving Jenny to chuckle behind him.

A few minutes later, Abigail Krimp came walking up with a disgusted look on her face. "Don't give Rollie nothing else to eat," she said. "He'll just throw it up. Again."

"Outside?" Jenny asked hopefully.

"No such luck."

Jenny shrugged. "Sorry, Abigail."

"No need. Rollie's gonna be sorry enough for himself and everybody else, too. I'm gonna let him lay in his own mess till he wakes up." Suddenly, she brightened. "Have you got a spare bowl for me? I found a nice place to eat outside."

Jenny fixed her right up, and Abigail walked away humming.

21

When Saul went home to check on Rachael and the boys, he found the children racing around the hardware store playing cowboys and wild Indians, and Rachael up, fully dressed, and opening the register for the day.

"Rachael!" he said, shocked. "Are you feeling well enough already?"

"And shouldn't I be the judge of that?" she replied. "I'm feeling fresh as a daisy, thank you, Saul. Don't you think you should turn the sign on the door around?"

"Certainly, certainly," he said, while he flipped the CLOSED sign around to OPEN. Was this the same Rachael he'd left this morning, still giddily half out of her mind on Morelli's potion and wobbling between consciousness and sleep?

"And?"

"And what, my dearest?"

"And what has brought on this rapid recovery? This morning, you were—"

She smiled as one of the boys dove between her feet and crawled out the other side of her skirt. "Not well. I know. But Dr. Morelli brought me the excellent news, and I suddenly felt so much better!"

"The excellent news? Rachael, talk English!"

Rachael cocked a hand on her hip and shook her head. "About Jason and the Apache. And you, my brave, brave Saul. Jason has the whole town to pick from, and it's my Saul he chooses to watch his back. I ask you, could I be more proud?"

It was Saul's turn to shake his head. "As long as I live, Rachael, I will never understand women."

She took the few steps to bring her around the counter and face-to-face with him. She touched his face. "And aren't you glad of that, my Sauly?"

Quickly, she rose on tiptoes to kiss his cheek, then went back behind the counter again, leaving him almost sputtering with embarrassment and surprise. She was usually so reticent!

"In front of the boys, Rachael?" he hissed.

"It was a kiss that started each of them," she chided, smiling softly. "And a kiss that will start the next one, when I'm healed. When time has passed."

Saul's shoulders hunched momentarily. "But do you think . . . ?" He sighed. Didn't she recall that this last fruitless delivery had very nearly killed her? "Women . . ."

"And what would you do without us, Saul?"

He sat on the nearest nail keg. "Live long, prosperous, worry-free lives, I'm guessing?"

She puckered her lips and shook her head. "Oh, Saul. You'd be unwashed, poorly fed, and very badly tempered."

"True, as usual," he said with a sigh.

She smiled. "Of course."

* * *

Colorado Gooding, well enough to be on his feet with the aid of a single crutch, navigated the crowded aisle of the livery and stepped out into the fresh air. Once in the clear, he took a deep breath and muttered, "Better."

He hadn't minded the stink of animals nearly so much as the stench of scorched wood. And the smell of the fellow next to him—gangrene, if he was any judge— hadn't been a real picnic, either.

He looked around himself on the street, looked at the wagons and the stove-up men, and the town's kids just beginning to wander out into the street.

Matt MacDonald was getting his buggy hitched up in front of the bank. Was he leaving without his missus? Colorado had passed Jenny on his way out of the stable, and Miss Megan, too. Matt's sister looked to be banged up pretty bad, and it seemed funny that Matt hadn't beaten a path in there right away, just to make certain she was still breathing.

But then again, he reminded himself, you never could count on Matt to do what was expected.

Unless, of course, it was puff up and carry on like a half-grown rooster, and then turn tail and run.

He couldn't spy Jason anywhere, but he spotted Mayor Kendall up the way a bit, and Randall Nordstrom. Rachael and Saul Cohen looked to be opening up their hardware store and Carrie Kendall was polishing the glass in the Kendalls' front window. Both Rachael and Carrie were right pretty women, he thought, and nice, too.

Wash Keough, who, up until this very moment, Colorado had figured was off somewhere happily digging for gold, lay on a cot outside, in the shade of the boardwalk overhang. His leg must be all busted up. At least, there was a splint bandaged tight to it, and one of those fancy plaster casts on his foot and ankle.

Wash waved at him, and he ambled on down with a big grin on his face.

"Glad to see you're still breathin'," Colorado said, and shook Wash's hand.

"You an' me both." Wash pushed himself up with one hand and shoved another pillow behind his head with the other. "Appears to me we been saved again."

"How'd that happen anyways?" Colorado asked. And Wash told him, told him as much as he knew anyhow. Or could remember.

"I'll be damned," was Colorado's most frequent comment.

"Got that right," was Wash's.

Neither man had planned on settling anywhere near here, but it seemed they'd both sunk in their toes and were going to live out their last days amid the folks of Fury. Which was a very good thing for the town, Jason had once told Colorado. Colorado had nodded sagely, though he hadn't had the slightest idea what Jason had been talking about.

Maybe he knew now, though. Maybe Jason had been talking about their collective need for cannon fodder.

That was one thing Colorado had learned over the years: that if he was good for anything, it was as a moving target. And he said so to Wash.

Wash laughed and slapped at his good knee. "Me,

too, I reckon! Least we know we're appreciated, Colorado. That's more than I've had in half the places I hung my hat before."

Colorado nodded. "Where's Jason?" he asked.

Wash pointed a finger. "Over in the jail, locked in and doped to the gills."

Colorado hiked a grizzled brow. "Locked in?"

Laughter was the reply, followed by: "Locked in for his own good. So's folks'll leave him alone for a while." Wash rifled in his vest pocket and finally brought out a pouch of tobacco. "You got papers?"

"Believe I do," Colorado said. Digging in his own pocket, he slouched back against the hitching rail.

It was good to have a smoke with a friend, and not have arrows coming at you from every which way.

It was good to relax.

"But he is a good fighter," said the brave traveling next to Cunning Dog. "He should be back by now."

Cunning Dog did not answer. He was twisted on his pony, scanning the northern horizon for any signs of his brother's return.

There were none.

"I warned Lone Wolf not to travel back to the town," said Cunning Dog after a long pause, "but he wished it so. It is an evil place, full of white devils. Only in the most evil of places could we lose so many brave men." He slowly shook his head. "There will be mourning in the camp when we reach it. There will be much sorrow."

His companion, a young brave called Mole Eyes,

said, "You tell me nothing new. I say someone should go back for Lone Wolf. Maybe we should all go back and teach those white devils whose land they have made their town on."

"You are justly named," said Cunning Dog, his tone low. "You are indeed blind."

Mole Eyes scowled at him, but Cunning Dog did not see it. His focus was straight ahead, between his pony's ears. "No one will go back. No one can save Lone Wolf except himself. It is how he wishes it to be."

"You are a coward, Cunning Dog."

In half a heartbeat, Cunning Dog had snatched the reins of Mole Eyes away and jerked both their ponies to a halt. Suddenly, Mole Eyes looked stricken.

Cunning Dog reeled in the pony until the warriors were so close that their knees touched. "Never say that to me again, or I will kill you. Do you understand?"

Too frightened to speak, Mole Eyes jerked his head up and down.

Cunning Dog stared at the younger warrior a moment longer, then cast his reins toward him with a sneer of disgust. Then he wheeled his pony and trotted on to take his place among the others, leaving Mole Eyes behind.

Blake sat on the tailgate of his wagon, next to his wife and infant son, watching the sun set over the town while he ate his stew. Yes, this was the place they'd stay. He'd talked to a number of the men, and they were all in agreement that the Indian menace was a thing of the past. According to them, they had killed so many Apache that they doubted there were enough left to mount a decent war party.

He nudged Laura with an elbow. "What do you think, honey?" he asked. "Could you be happy here?"

She beamed at him. "Ecstatically," she said, and he knew she'd been thinking along the same lines that he had.

He nodded. "Then here's where we'll stay."

He began to make plans for his church.

Jason opened his eyes just a crack.

"Well," said Jenny in a satisfied voice. "Finally going to spend some time with us, are you?"

Jason grunted.

"And don't try to tell me you're going to go back to sleep, mister. It's four o'clock in the morning. You've been sleeping forever!"

"What?"

"You heard me. Four in the morning, you lazy thing."

Jason tried to sit up, but he'd forgotten the knife wound in his shoulder and pushed up with the wrong hand. "Crap," he muttered as a stabbing pain went through his shoulder and down his arm.

"Be careful of that side," Jenny said, rearranging his covers matter-of-factly. "Dr. Morelli said that wound of yours might reopen if you got too rough with it." She smoothed the blanket and sat back down beside his cot.

He didn't remember being brought to the jail. He wondered if it was because his house was still full of other people. He wondered if Matt MacDonald had left town, and if he'd made a scene with Jenny.

He said, "Matt gone?"

Jenny's brow furrowed. "Yes. The son of a—well, you know what—he left without even trying to find me. Or his own sister, for goodness sake!"

Jason wasn't surprised. "How's Megan?"

"Oh, she's gonna be fine, and Morelli says the scar won't show at all."

"Don't care about the scar," he said.

"I know it wouldn't mean anything to you, but Megan's a girl. Things like that are important."

He snorted despite himself.

"Oh, you know what I mean." She gave his side a little smack, and he figured he must be pretty much on the way to mended for Jenny to be that playfully rough with him.

But he yelped anyway.

And Jenny's eyes practically bugged from her head. "Jason! Are you all right? I didn't hurt you, did I?"

This time, he pushed himself up with his good arm and tackled her unexpectedly, pulling her across the covers. At last, giggling and crying what her mother had dubbed "laughing tears," she broke free from his tickling fingers.

"Honestly, Jason!" she finally managed to get out. "Sometimes you can be such a stinker!"

He blurted a guffaw. "Me?" It crossed his mind to mention the prime example of stinkerdom—her having married Matt MacDonald—but he thought better of it. Instead, he said, "I think you're the one who's a . . . never mind. I'm a gentleman."

Jenny's hands balled into fists and she rose up on tip-toes. "Are you saying that I'm no lady?"

Jason, having just fought his way through a judgment day of sorts, had no intention of inviting a new one. But he couldn't help saying, "You said it, not me."

Quicker than he could see, Jenny grabbed one of the pillows from under his head and began to mercilessly pummel him—avoiding, he noticed, anyplace where he was really, truly hurt.

So he made a lunge toward her, changing his position on the cot quite suddenly. And taking an unintentional blow directly on his bad shoulder.

"YOUCH!" he cried, gripping it and falling back fast.

"Jason! Oh, no, poor Jason, I didn't mean it, really, I didn't—" Jenny was suddenly sobbing and plucking at his shoulder dressing.

He brushed her away. "Don't fuss at me. I'll be all right."

And then it occurred to him that yes, this time he really could be all right! The town's Indian problem was solved, wasn't it? Ward would make as good a sheriff as he had a deputy, once he got used to the idea. His sister, Jenny, had at last made a clean break with Matt Mac-Donald—the divorce would be fast and efficient. And he'd practically arranged a match for her with Ward.

He could leave. He could really, finally leave.

He heaved a most happy sigh, which Jenny took for permission to start talking again.

"Of course, you'll have to be careful with that shoulder for a bit. Dr. Morelli said you very nearly lost all use of that arm."

What?

"And then there's the Mortons. They were completely burnt out, you know. Salmon Kendall and somebody else rode up there this afternoon. He said to tell you that they left the livestock where they found it, and just hauled hay and feed out to them. But they brought the dog back to town. That means our house, Jason."

He pulled the pillow up over his face.

"Ward says they want to go home, but he told them you had to give them permission to leave town, plus which, they don't have a home to go to."

"Aw, crud," he muttered as his happy thoughts of leaving town evaporated.

"And a small train of new people pulled in today. Looks like they're going to stay, too, at least some of them. We've got a new reverend—the Reverend Blake—and he drinks beer. That's what Ward says anyway. I met his wife, Laura. She's really nice."

"A new reverend?"

"And then there's poor Megan," Jenny went on heedlessly. "The poor thing's concerned that her misfortune will leave her disfigured, and therefore not good enough for you, and—"

Jason held up a hand. "Stop."

"What?"

"Stop," he repeated wearily. "You've already told me. You win. The town wins. It always does, doesn't it?"

"What are you talking about?"

"Nothing. Go away, Jenny."

"But Jason . . ."

"Not tonight, okay? Let me go back to sleep and we'll talk later. In the real morning. When the sun's up, for instance."

"All right then," Jenny said, her tone of voice telling him that she'd given up. For now at least. He heard her footsteps cross to the cell door, then to the office door, heard the door unlatch and open. "Good night, Jason. Sleep tight."

He heard his deceased mother's voice, so much like Jenny's, echo warmly but hollowly through his head: "Don't let the bedbugs bite."

Jenny closed the door behind her, and was gone.

"Aw, crud," he muttered before he fell asleep again.

1

Willow Creek, Colorado

A heavy, booming thunder rolled over the breaks, and gray veils of rain hung down from ominous black clouds that crowded the hills. Though it had not yet reached him, the storm was moving quickly, and Smoke Jensen took a poncho from his saddlebag and slipped it on to be prepared for the impending downpour.

Smoke was on his way to Denver, and he was butt-sore from riding. Hunkering down from an approaching storm, he saw the little town of Willow Creek rising before him. The town had no more than half-a-dozen commercial buildings, and about three dozen houses.

Smoke leaned forward and patted his horse on the neck.

"What do you say that we find us a place to ride this storm out?" Smoke asked his horse. Often on long, lonely rides, Smoke wanted to hear a human voice, even if it was his own. Talking to his horse provided him with an excuse for talking aloud, without really talking to himself.

"A livery for you, and maybe supper and a beer for me," he continued in his one-sided conversation.

The first few drops of rain had just started when Smoke rode in through the big open door of the Jim Bob Corral. His nostrils were assailed with the pungent but familiar smell of hay, horseflesh, and horse manure. To a city person the odor might be unpleasant, but to Smoke, the aroma was almost comforting. Smoke took off his poncho and rolled it up. He had just finished tying it back onto his saddle when a boy of about sixteen appeared, having come from somewhere deep in the shadows of the barn.

"You wantin' to board your horse here, mister?" the boy asked.

"Yes," Smoke answered. "Find a dry place for him, rub him down, and give him oats." Smoke gave the boy a dollar.

"How long?" the boy asked.

"Just tonight."

"Then it's only a quarter," the boy said. "I'll get your change."

"You keep the change," Smoke said. "Just take extra care of my horse."

A broad smile spread across the boy's face. "Mister, the folks stayin' over to the Dunn Hotel won't be gettin' no better treatment than this here horse."

"I appreciate that," Smoke said.

Smoke looked across the street at the saloon.

"Do they serve food in the saloon?" he asked.

"Yes, sir, and it's good food too," the boy said. "My ma cooks there."

Smoke smiled. "Then I know I will enjoy it."

The rain was coming down pretty steadily now as Smoke hurried across the street for the saloon. Stepping inside, he took off his hat, then poured water from the crown as he looked around. For a town so small, the saloon was surprisingly full. It even had a piano, at which a piano player was grinding away in the back.

More than half the patrons in the saloon turned to look at him, and as they realized he was not a local, even more turned to see who the stranger in their midst was.

The barkeep moved toward him when Smoke stepped up to the bar.

"Hope you ain't put out none by ever'one lookin' at you, but we don't get a lot of visitors here, especially on a night like this."

"A night like this is what drove me here," Smoke replied.

The bartender chuckled. "Yes, sir, I see what you mean. What's your pleasure?"

"I'd like a beer."

"Yes, sir, one beer comin' up."

A moment later, the bartender put a mug of golden beer with a frothy head in front of Smoke. Smoke blew off some of the head, then took a long swallow. After a full day of riding, the beer tasted very good to him, and he took another deep drink before he turned his back to the bar to have a look around the place that called itself The Gilded Lily.

A card game was going on in the corner and Smoke watched it for a few minutes while he drank his beer.

Smoke's peripheral vision caught someone coming in through the back door, and turning, he saw a tall, broad-shouldered man wearing a badge. Because he had just come in from the rain, water was dripping from the lawman's sweeping mustache.

"I'm lookin' for a man named Emerson Pardeen," the man announced to the room."

One of the cardplayers stood up slowly, then turned to face the man with the badge.

"I'm Emerson Pardeen. Who the hell are you?"

"The name is Buck Wheeler. *Marshal* Buck Wheeler," he added, coming down hard on the word *Marshal*.

"Yeah? Well, what do you want with me?"

"I'm taking you back to Dodge City to stand trial for the murder of Jason Tibbs."

"Dodge City is in Kansas. This is Colorado. You got no jurisdiction here."

"Maybe I should've told you I'm a United States marshal," Wheeler added. "I've got jurisdiction everywhere."

"Yeah? Well, Mr. United States Marshal Buck Wheeler, I ain't goin' back to Dodge City with you," Pardeen said.

"Oh, you're going back all right," Wheeler said. "Either sitting in your saddle, or belly-down over it."

Realizing that a gunfight was very likely, the others who had been sitting at the table jumped up and moved out of the way, a couple of them moving so quickly that their chairs fell over.

The marshal pulled his gun and pointed it at Pardeen. "Now, shuck out of that gun belt, slow and easy like," he ordered.

Pardeen shook his head. "No, I don't think so. I think maybe I'm just goin' to call you on this one."

"Whatever you say, Pardeen. Whatever you say," the marshal replied.

Smoke, like the others, was watching the drama unfold when he heard a soft squeaking sound as if weight were being put down on a loose board. The sound caused him to look up toward the top of the stairs. When he did so, he saw a man standing there, aiming a shotgun at the back of the marshal.

"Marshal, there's a gun at your back!" Smoke shouted. Concurrent with Smoke's warning, the man wielding the shotgun turned it toward Smoke.

"You sorry son of a bitch!" he shouted.

Smoke had no choice then. He dropped his beer and pulled his pistol, firing just as the man at the top of the stairs squeezed his own trigger. The shotgun boomed loudly. The heavy charge of buckshot tore a large hole in the top and side of the bar, right where Smoke had been standing. Some of the shot hit the whiskey bottles in front of the mirror, and one of the nude statues behind the bar. Like shrapnel from an exploding bomb, pieces of glass flew everywhere. The mirror fell except for a few jagged shards, which hung in place where the mirror had been, reflecting distorted images of the dramatic scene playing out before it.

Smoke's single shot had not missed, and the man with the shotgun dropped his weapon. His eyes rolled up in his head and he fell, twisting around so that he slid down the stairs on his back headfirst, following his clattering shotgun to the ground floor. The wielder of the shotgun lay at the foot of the stairs with his head on the floor and his legs splayed apart, stretching back up the bottom four steps. His sightless eyes were open and staring up toward the ceiling.

The sound of the two gunshots had riveted everyone's attention to that exchange, and while their attention was diverted from him, Pardeen took the opportunity to go for his own gun. Suddenly, the saloon was filled with the roar of another gunshot as Pardeen fired at the marshal who had confronted him.

Marshal Wheeler had made the fatal mistake of being diverted by the gunplay between Smoke and the shotgun shooter. Pardeen's bullet struck the marshal in the forehead and the impact of it knocked him back on a nearby table. The marshal lay belly up on the table with his head hanging down on the far side while blood dripped from the hole in his forehead to form a puddle below him. His gun fell from his lifeless hand and clattered to the floor. Pardeen then swung his pistol toward Smoke.

"Mister, this isn't my fight," Smoke said. "We can end it here and now." Smoke put his pistol back in its holster.

Realizing that he now had the advantage, a big smile spread across Pardeen's face. "Oh, it's goin' to end all right," Pardeen said. "'Cause I aim to end it right now." Pardeen cocked his pistol.

Those who were looking on in morbid fascination were surprised by what happened next, because even as Pardeen was cocking his pistol, Smoke drew and fired. His bullet caught Pardeen in the center of his chest and Pardeen went down. He sat up, then clutched his hand over the wound as blood spilled between his fingers.

"How the hell did you do that?" he asked. He coughed once, then he fell back, dead.

"What's goin' on in here?" a voice asked. "What's all the shootin'?"

When Smoke turned toward the sound of the voice, he saw a man dripping water onto the floor as he stood just inside the open door. Because the man was standing in the shadows, Smoke couldn't quite make out his features.

"Step into the light so I can see you," Smoke said.

"Mister, do you know who you are talking to?" the man in the door asked.

Smoke pulled the hammer back, and his pistol made a deadly metallic click as the sear engaged the cylinder. "Doesn't much matter who I'm talking to. In about one second you'll be dead if you don't step into the light."

This time the man moved as ordered. Doing so enabled Smoke to see the badge on the man's shirt, and he let the hammer down on his pistol, then dropped it back into his holster.

"Sorry, Sheriff," Smoke said. "I didn't know you were the law."

"What happened here?"

"I'll tell you what happened," one of the other cardplayers said.

"Who are you?"

"The name is Corbett." Corbett pointed to Smoke. "This here fella just kilt three men. He kilt the marshal, Eddie Phillips, and Emerson Pardeen."

The sheriff made a grunting sound. "Now you tell me, Corbett, just why would this fella kill the marshal *and*

Pardeen? Marshal Wheeler stopped by my office not ten minutes ago to tell me he was here to arrest Pardeen, so I know it isn't very likely that Marshal Wheeler and Pardeen would be on the same side in this fracas."

"Hell, Sheriff, I don't know why he done it. Maybe you need to ask him."

"All right, I'll ask him," the sheriff said. "Did you kill all three of these men, mister?"

"No. I only killed two of them," Smoke replied.

Inexplicably, the sheriff chuckled. "I see. You just killed two of them. So that makes you what? One-third innocent?"

"One hundred percent innocent," Smoke replied. "I only killed the ones who were trying to kill me. And in my book that is self-defense."

"He's lyin', Sheriff," Corbett said. "He kilt Phillips and Pardeen in cold blood."

"Oh, so now you are saying he only killed two of them?"

"In cold blood, yes," Corbett said.

"Corbett is the one who is lyin', Sheriff," the bartender said. "This fella is telling the truth. Eddie Phillips shot first. He was standin' up there at the head of the stairs holdin' a scattergun pointed at the marshal's back. This fella shouted a warnin' to the marshal, and Phillips turned the gun on him. Take a look at the bar here, and you'll see what I'm talkin' about. Hell, it was a wonder I wasn't kilt my ownself. Then Pardeen kilt Marshal Wheeler and swung his gun around toward this fella, tellin' him he was fixin' to kill him too. And what happened then, you ain't goin' to believe."

"Try me," the sheriff said.

"Well, sir, this here fella had already put his gun away. Pardeen had the drop on him, and was pullin' back the hammer when this fella drew and shot him. Damn'dest thing I ever seen."

The sheriff stroked his chin as he looked at Smoke. "Is what he saying true?"

Smoke nodded. "It's like the barkeep said. Pardeen was about to shoot me."

"Pardeen wasn't about to shoot him," Corbett said. "He was just goin' to hold him for killin' Phillips and the marshal."

"Hold him?"

"Yeah, Pardeen was goin' to hold him until you got here," Corbett said.

Several in the saloon laughed then.

"Tell you what, Sheriff. You arrest him, I'll testify against him at his trial."

"Corbett," the sheriff said. "I'm not aware that there is any paper out on you, but that might be because I haven't looked hard enough."

Corbett's eyes narrowed. "You ain't goin' to find any paper on me, Sheriff. The one you should arrest is this fella."

The sheriff looked around the saloon at the other patrons, who were still watching the drama.

"Anyone in here back up what Corbett is saying?" the sheriff asked.

Several responded at once.

"He ain't tellin' it the way I seen it," one of the other

customers said. "I seen it the same way the bartender told it."

"That's the way it looked to me, too," another said.

"Yeah, ever' word the bartender said is the gospel."

The sheriff held up his hand. "So what I'm hearin' is, nobody backs up Corbett's version of the story?"

Everyone was quiet, and the sheriff looked at Corbett. "Looks like a clear case of self-defense to me," he said.

Corbett looked at Smoke. "Pardeen was my friend," he said. "I don't like the way you shot him down like that. Maybe I'll just settle the score myself."

"No!" the sheriff said. "There's been enough killin' for one night."

"What's your name, mister?" Corbett asked.

"Jensen. Kirby Jensen. But most folks just call me Smoke."

There was a collective gasp from everyone in the saloon.

"Smoke Jensen," one unidentified speaker said. "No wonder he could do what he done. Ain't nobody nowhere no faster'n Smoke Jensen."

"Are you the Smoke Jensen from over by Big Rock?" the sheriff asked. "That Smoke Jensen?"

"I have a ranch just outside Big Rock, yes," Smoke replied. He knew that the sheriff was trying to determine if he was "the" Smoke Jensen, but humility prevented him from elaborating.

"I'll be damned," the sheriff said. "What are you doing in Willow Creek?"

"I'm just passing through, on my way to Denver," Smoke said.

The sheriff looked over at Corbett, who had also recognized the name.

"Corbett, you still want to settle accounts with this fella?"

Corbett stroked his chin nervously. "Uh, no, Sheriff, it's like you said, there's been enough killin' for one night."

Corbett pointed at Smoke. "But I think maybe you ought to know that Pardeen has a brother named Quince. He ain't goin' to like it that you kilt Emerson and one of these days you'n him are goin' to run across each other." Corbett smiled a dry, humorless smile. "And when you two do run into each other, well, I would like to be there to see it."

"That wouldn't be a threat now, would it, Corbett?" the sheriff asked.

"No threat," Corbett said. "Just a friendly warnin', so to speak."

"There ain't nothin' about you friendly," the sheriff said. "If I was you, Corbett, I'd leave town right now."

"In case you ain't noticed, Sheriff, there's a storm goin' on out there," Corbett said.

"Because I'm going to go back to my office and look for a dodger on you," the sheriff continued, as if he had not even heard Corbett. "And if I can't find one, I may just come back and arrest you anyway."

Corbett glared at Smoke and the sheriff for a moment longer. Then he picked up his hat and started toward the door. "I'll be goin' now."

"Wait!" the sheriff called after him.

Corbett stopped and looked back.

"What about your pards?" the sheriff asked, pointing to Pardeen and Phillips.

"What about 'em?" Corbett replied.

"Are you just goin' to walk out and leave them layin' here? Aren't you going to wait until the undertaker comes so you can make burial arrangements?" the sheriff asked.

"Hell, they ain't either one of 'em my kin. That means they ain't my responsibility," Corbett said. "Just put 'em anywhere."

"I see. Friendship don't mean that much to you, does it?" the sheriff asked.

"They was my friends when they was alive. They're dead," Corbett said, as if somehow that justified his in-difference to them. He pushed through the batwing doors and walked out into the pouring rain.

"Are you planning on staying in town for long, Mr. Jensen?" the sheriff asked.

"The name's Smoke, Sheriff," Smoke said in a friendly tone. "I had only planned to stay the night, just long enough to ride out the storm. But I reckon I can stay a bit longer if you think that's necessary."

The sheriff looked at the bodies still lying on the saloon floor. "No," he said, shaking his head. "There are enough witnesses here to verify what happened. I see no need for getting a judge to come this far just for an in-quest that we know how it's going to turn out."

"If you do need me for anything, just get in touch with Sheriff Carson in Big Rock."

"I'm sure there won't be a need for that," the sheriff replied. "Oh, but Smoke, there's one thing Corbett said that you should take to heart."

"What's that?"

"Quince Pardeen. Do you know him?"

Smoke shook his head. "I've heard his name, but I can't say that I know him."

"He's good with a gun, but that ain't the thing that makes him so dangerous. What makes him dangerous is the fact that he is a killer, and he don't particular care how he kills. You look out for him."

"I will, Sheriff," Smoke replied. "And thanks for the warning."

2

Denver wasn't the largest city Smoke had ever seen, but it was the largest city in Colorado and as Smoke rode down Wynkoop Street, he had to maneuver his horse from side to side in order to negotiate his way through the heavy traffic of coaches, carriages, and wagons.

There was a large banner stretched across the street, and looking up, Smoke smiled when he saw the name.

COLORADO HONORS MATT JENSEN

This was a proud moment for Smoke, having Matt honored by the State of Colorado.

As a young boy, Matt Cavanaugh had run away from an orphanage, and would have died had Smoke not found him shivering in a snowbank in the mountains. Smoke took him to his cabin and nursed him back to health.

It had been Smoke's intention to keep the boy around only until he had recovered, but Matt wound up staying with Smoke until he reached manhood. During the time

Matt had lived with Smoke, he became Smoke's student, learning everything from Smoke that Smoke had learned from Preacher many years earlier, including the most important lesson of all, how to be a man of honor.

By the time Matt reached the age of eighteen, he was skilled in everything from the use of weapons to fighting, tracking, hunting, and camping. Feeling that the time was right, he left to go on his own. Smoke did not have the slightest hesitancy over sending him out, because Matt had become one of the most capable young men Smoke had ever seen.

Just before Matt left, he surprised Smoke by asking permission to take Smoke's last name as his own. Smoke was not only honored by the request, he was touched, and to this day there was a bond between them that was as close as any familial bond could be.*

Smoke and Matt had shared their time together long before Smoke married Sally, and long before his two most loyal hands, Pearlie and Cal, had come to work at Sugarloaf. But Sally understood the bond between the Smoke and Matt, and it was she who suggested that Smoke go to Denver for the ceremony.

After getting a room at the hotel, Smoke took a bath and put on a suit, then went downstairs and walked through the lobby to a large ballroom that was being used as a reception hall. Through the open door of the room, he could see several well-dressed men and women standing around, laughing and talking.

*The Last Mountain Man

A large man was standing near the open door, looking out into the lobby. By the man's demeanor and by the expression on his face, Smoke could see that he was not a guest at the reception, but was a guard. The guard came toward Smoke, shaking his head and with his hand extended.

"Sir, this is a closed reception," the guard said.

"That's good," Smoke said. "It shouldn't be open for just anyone. Why, there's no telling what kind of disreputable figure might try to come in."

"You don't understand, sir," the guard said. "I'm talking about you. You can't come in here."

"Wait a minute. Are you calling me a disreputable figure?"

"No, sir, I'm just telling you that this is a closed reception and unless you have a personal invitation from the governor, you cannot come in."

"Well, the gentleman being honored and I are old friends," Smoke said.

"Do you have an invitation?"

"No."

The guard smiled triumphantly. "Well, if you were old friends, you would have an invitation now, wouldn't you? I'm sorry, sir, but you can't come in. I'm going to have to ask you to leave."

"Why don't we just ask the man being honored?" Smoke suggested. He started into the room.

"Sir, if you don't leave now, I am going to personally throw you out of here!"

Smoke looked at the guard. The guard was a big man, and it was obvious that he could handle himself. But at the same time Smoke was looking over the guard, the guard was taking stock of Smoke, and Smoke could see by the expression in his face that he wasn't looking forward to any encounter with someone Smoke's size.

Smoke sighed. The guard was just doing his job.

"All right," Smoke said. "I don't want to cause any trouble." He pointed to the lobby. "I'll wait out here. I would appreciate it, though, if you would tell Matt Jensen that Smoke is here."

At that moment, the governor happened to glance over toward the door and saw Smoke standing in the door. Breaking into a wide smile, the governor came over to extend a personal greeting.

"Smoke Jensen," Governor John Long Routt said, extending his hand. "How good to see you."

"Hello, John," Smoke replied, returning the smile.

"Governor, this man doesn't have an invitation," the guard said.

"Really? Well, don't worry about it, Mitchell," the governor said. "Mr. Jensen and I are old friends."

"Oh. Mr. Jensen, I'm sorry I didn't know. I hope you don't take offense."

"Don't be sorry, my friend," Smoke said. "You were just doing your job. And if I may say so, you were doing it quite well."

"Uh, yes, sir. Thank you, sir. But you should'a said you were a friend of the governor. You said you were a friend of the man being honored."

"Indeed he is, Mitchell," Governor Routt said. "In fact, he is much more than a friend. Perhaps you didn't catch his last name. It is Jensen."

"Jensen? Oh, you mean like Matt Jensen, the man getting the award tonight?"

"Yes," Governor Routt said. "Come with me, Smoke, I'm sure Matt is looking for you."

Smoke shook his head. "I doubt it," he said. "I didn't tell him I was coming. I wanted to surprise him."

"Oh. Well, that is even better. Come along."

Smoke followed the governor through a cloud of aromatic tobacco and pipe smoke. He saw Matt before Matt saw him. It was easy to pick Matt out from the crowd. His young protégé stood over six feet tall with broad shoulders and narrow hips. His blond hair seemed even more yellow than Smoke remembered.

Matt didn't see Smoke right away because he had his back turned and he was surrounded by almost half-a-dozen very beautiful women, each woman vying for his attention. As Smoke approached, the women broke out into laughter over some story Matt was telling.

"You always were able to spin a good yarn," Smoke said.

Recognizing Smoke's voice, Matt turned toward his mentor with a broad smile on his face.

"Smoke! What are you doing here?"

"You are getting an award from the governor, aren't you?" Smoke replied. "I had to be here."

Matt took Smoke's hand in his, and the two shook hands and clasped each other on the shoulder.

"Ladies, this is Smoke Jensen," Matt said.

"Did you say Jensen?" one of the women asked.

"I sure did."

"Is he your brother?" another asked.

Matt nodded. "Yes indeed," Matt said. "Smoke is my brother."

There was a dinner after the reception, and though Smoke offered to leave, he was persuaded to stay when he learned that the governor had made special arrangements for him at the head table. When all were seated, Governor Routt tapped his spoon on the crystal goblet. The clear ringing sound could be heard above all the laughter and conversation, and it had the desired effect of silencing the guests.

"Ladies and gentlemen, it is my distinct honor and privilege tonight to host this banquet in honor of Matthew Jensen, one of Colorado's leading citizens.

"Last winter during an attempted train robbery, some bandits killed both the engineer and the fireman of the Midnight Flyer. Now, the dead man's throttle is supposed to stop the train anytime the engineer is incapacitated, but it failed, and rather than stopping the train as the bandits planned, their action caused a runaway train. Matt Jensen was a passenger on that train. And while he knew nothing about the attempted holdup, he did realize, rather quickly, that the train was in great danger. He knew also that, somehow, he would have to get to the engine.

"The only way for him to get to the engine was to crawl along the top of the swaying, ice-covered cars on a train that was speeding through the dark at sixty miles per hour. Matt finally managed to reach the engine and stop the train, just before it rounded a sharp turn. Had he not succeeded, the speed they were traveling would have sent the train and all one hundred and thirty-one passengers over the side of a mountain to a sure and certain death."

The governor paused in his speech long enough to enable the crowd to react with exclamations of awe and wonder at Matt's skill and bravery. The crowd did just as he expected, and the governor waited until it was quiet again before he continued with his proclamation.

"And now, as governor of the State of Colorado, I hereby issue this proclamation declaring this day to be officially entered into the State historical records as Matthew Jensen Day."

The presentation was greeted with applause and cheers for Matt, who, despite the shouts of "Speech!" managed only to mumble his thanks.

Following the reception and dinner, Smoke was surprised by the number of people who, after congratulating Matt, came to shake his own hand.

At breakfast the next morning, Smoke commented on his surprise over the number of people who had made a special effort to greet him.

"You shouldn't be surprised," Matt replied. "Surely you know that you are one of the best-known men in the entire state of Colorado. Why, if you ran for governor today, I've no doubt but that you would be elected."

Smoke chuckled. "Don't tell John that," he said. "Though he has no need to worry. I have no intention of ever entering politics," he said. "But maybe you should. You are getting quite an enviable reputation yourself, and you are still young enough—why, you could have a very successful political career."

"Thanks, but no, thanks," Matt replied, clearly uncomfortable with any such suggestion. Clearing his throat, he changed the subject. "How is Sally?"

"Sally sends her love."

"You tell her that I send mine as well," Matt said.

"I'll do that," Smoke said, putting some money on the table as he stood.

"No," Matt said resolutely. He picked the money up and gave it back. "I'm buying breakfast."

Smoke picked up the bill and laughed. "All right," he said. "But don't you think for one moment that a measly breakfast is going to pay me back for all the meals I furnished you when you were a snot-nosed kid."

Matt laughed as well and walked to the door with his friend. It was always like this when the two encountered each other. Matt had never made an effort to dissuade him from leaving, nor had he ever put forth any offer to join him. Each man was supremely confident in his own life, and in the absolute certainty that their friendship would remain strong, despite lengthy and distant separation.

"Smoke?" Matt called as Smoke mounted his horse.

Smoke swung into the saddle, then patted his horse on the neck before he responded.

"Yes?"

"You take care, you hear? You're the only family I have."

Smoke touched the brim of his hat and nodded. "I'll do that, Matt," he replied.

* * *

As Smoke reached the edge of Denver, he had to stop at the track to wait for a train to pass. He sat in his saddle and watched the windows slide by, nodding at a couple of the passengers who had nodded at him.

One of the passengers in the train was Trent Williams, and though Williams did not acknowledge the cowboy who sat on his horse alongside the track, he did see him. Then, just after they passed the cowboy, Williams heard the hiss and squeal of the brakes. As the train started to slow, Williams took an envelope from his inside jacket pocket and pulled a well-read letter from the envelope, opened it, then read it again.

Dear Mr. Williams

Your offer to buy fifty-one percent of the Miners Bank and Trust has been received, and our board asks that you come to Denver to present your proposal in person.

We are in agreement that we would like to have you run our bank, but there is some concern as to whether we should turn over absolute control to one man, as would be the case if you were to acquire fifty-one percent of the stock. We look forward to meeting you and to discuss, at length, the details of the sale. I will meet you at the depot to take you to the bank, where the board meeting will take place. In order that you may recognize

*me, I will be wearing a red feather in the band of
my hat.*

> *Sincerely,*
> *Vernon Bess*

Williams put the letter away as the train screeched to a
halt. When he stepped out onto the platform, he saw a
man wearing a hat with a red feather in the band.

"Mr. Bess?" he asked.

The man smiled and extended his hand. "Yes, you are
Mr. Williams, I presume?"

"I am."

"I have a carriage here," Bess said. "The board meeting will be held at ten o'clock this morning. Do you have
luggage?"

"I do, yes."

Bess made a motion toward the driver of the carriage,
and the driver went to retrieve Williams's luggage.

"I think you will have no trouble with the board. As
president of the Bank of Salcedo in Wyoming, you have
just the kind of experience that can make a success of
our bank. Although I must say that at first the board members were a little put off with your insistence on owning
fifty-one percent. I think you will have to explain why you
feel that is necessary."

"It is absolutely necessary if I am to make a success
of the bank," Williams said.

"I'm sure you will be able to make your case satisfac-
torily," Bess replied.

* * *

The board, which was made up of investors and businessmen from Denver, had gathered at the bank for the meeting, and they greeted Vernon Bess when he arrived.

"Gentlemen of the board, it is my pleasure to introduce Mr. Trent Williams. As you know, Mr. Williams is president of the Bank of Salcedo. I have done research on that bank and find that it is one of the most successful and fiscally sound banks in all of Wyoming. I believe him to be just the man we are looking for."

Williams acknowledged the introduction, then spoke to the board for a few minutes about his plans for the Miners Bank and Trust. Then he asked if there were any questions.

"Mr. Williams, why do you insist on buying fifty-one percent of the bank?" one of the board members asked.

"If I am going to make this bank successful, I must have total freedom of operation," Williams explained. "With fifty-one percent, I will not have to be bound by any restrictions placed on me by the board."

"So, what you are saying is that you want to just make us powerless."

"Well, I wouldn't put it quite that way," Williams replied. "I will, of course, be open to any suggestions the board might have."

"I don't know if I can go along with that. After all, I have a lot of money invested in this bank. What if you are wrong and the bank fails?"

"I will have a lot more money invested than you," Williams said. "That means I have even more incentive than you to make the bank succeed."

"Elmer, think about it," Bess said to the hesitant

board member. "He's not going to invest fifty thousand dollars, then let the bank fail."

"I agree," one of the other board members said. "If Mr. Williams needs freedom of action to save the bank, I say let's give it to him. God knows we haven't been doing very well ourselves. And this way, we'll be able to recoup some of our money while still maintaining an investment. If he succeeds in making the bank successful, we will congratulate ourselves for having made such a sound decision."

"How soon can we expect the fifty thousand dollars?" Elmer asked Williams.

"I will have to return to Salcedo and put my affairs in order there," Williams said. "It would not be fair to my employers to leave without giving adequate notice."

"An honorable thing for you to do," Bess said. "All the more reason I believe we should accept the proposal. I now call for a vote."

The board voted to accept the proposal with even Elmer voting "aye." Williams accepted the congratulations of the board, then left the bank to walk down to the hotel.

Before registering at the hotel, he stopped at the Western Union Office to send a telegram.

UNDERSTAND YOU HAVE NEED FOR CATTLE STOP
PLEASE ADVISE ME OF BEST PRICE PER HEAD STOP
REPLY TRENT WILLIAMS SALCEDO WYOMING
TERRITORY STOP

3

Smoke had been home for two weeks when he was awakened one morning by the aroma of cooking breakfast. When he got dressed and went into the kitchen, he saw that Sally was preparing a veritable feast: eggs, bacon, biscuits, gravy, and fresh-baked bear claws. Pearlie and Cal were already in the dining room, drinking coffee and looking on hungrily.

"You boys are up early," Smoke said, speaking to his two longtime and most loyal hands.

"How could I sleep with Pealie's stomach growlin' so?" Cal asked.

"Oh? Was your stomach growling, Pearlie?" Smoke teased.

"How could it not be?" Pearlie replied. "There I was, sleepin' out there in the bunkhouse all peaceful like, when all of a sudden I started smellin' the most wonderful smells. You doggone right my stomach started growlin'."

"So, me'n Pearlie come in here and seen Miz Sally just cookin' away," Cal said.

"So, Miz Sally, ain't it about ready?" Pearlie asked. "All them smells got me so hungry I can't hardly stand it."

Sally sighed. "Pearlie, I swear, your grammar is so atrocious that it makes me cringe."

"Well, yes'm, I mean bein' as you was a schoolmarm 'n all a'fore you and Smoke married up, well, I reckon it'd be only natural that you wouldn't think I talk all that good," Pearlie said.

Sally put her hands over her ears. "Ahhh!" she said. "Smoke, shoot him! Shoot him right now before he says another word!"

"No, ma'am!" Pearlie said. "Leastwise, not till I've et some of this here breakfast."

Sally laughed, and shook her head. "You are incorrigible," she said.

"Yes'm, I reckon I am," Pearlie said. "I'm hungry, too."

"Go sit at the table, all of you. I'll bring it to you."

After the huge breakfast, when Smoke finished his coffee, Sally jumped up from the table and refilled his cup.

"You're being awfully nice, Sally," Smoke said.

"Can't I be nice to my husband if I feel like it?" Sally replied with a sweet smile.

"You'll get no argument from me," Smoke said, returning the smile.

"I swear, Miz Sally, if this ain't about the best breakfast I done ever et anywhere," Pearlie said.

"Ha!" Cal said. "It's come to my mind, Pearlie, that anything you eat is the best thing you ever ate."

"Well, yeah, I do like to eat, there ain't no denyin' that. But this here breakfast is particular good."

Cal nodded. "I'll have to agree with you on that. Why the big feed, Miz Sally?"

"No particular reason," Sally answered.

Smoke stared at his wife over the rim of his coffee cup. Seeing his intense stare, Sally looked away.

"Another bear claw, darling?" she asked.

"What is it, Sally?" Smoke asked. "What is going on?"

"What makes you think something is going on?"

"Because I know you, Sally. We're married, remember?"

"All right, I'll tell you," Sally replied.

Sally poured herself a cup of coffee, then sat back down before she answered.

"Do you remember the big winter freeze we had a couple of years ago? We lost over eighty percent of our herd. Do you remember that?"

"Of course I remember that," Smoke said. "We not only lost our herd, we almost lost Sugarloaf."

Sally reached back to the sideboard and got a small book, which she slid across the table to Smoke.

"What is that?" Smoke asked.

"It's the *Farmer's Almanac,*" Sally said. "According to the *Almanac,* this winter is going to be as bad as that one was."

"Oh, that's bad," Pearlie said. "That's really bad."

"And that's why the big breakfast?" Smoke asked. "We are celebrating the fact that we are going to have another bad winter?"

Sally shook her head. "No, we are celebrating the fact that a bad winter isn't going to be as big a problem for us this year."

Smoke drummed his fingers on the table. "What makes you think it won't be a problem?"

"After that last big freeze, you built shelter areas, remember?"

"Of course I remember. But we can only shelter about half of our herd."

"That's all we'll need to shelter," Sally said.

"Sally, it won't put Sugarloaf in danger like the last freeze-up, but do you have any idea how much money it would cost us to lose three thousand head."

"Just over one hundred thousand dollars," Sally said easily.

"What?"

"It would cost us just over one hundred thousand dollars to lose three thousand head. But we won't lose them if we sell them," Sally said.

Smoke shook his head. "You might be right, but if everyone is in the same situation, we won't be able to sell them."

"I know where we can sell them," Sally said.

"Where?"

"We can sell them to Mr. Colin Abernathy."

Smoke shook his head in confusion. "I don't know anyone named Colin Abernathy. He's not a local rancher. Is he an absentee owner?"

"Mr. Abernathy is the Indian agent for all the Cheyenne in Wyoming Territory. He needs the beef to get the Indians through the winter."

"Wait a minute. Did you say all the Cheyenne in Wyoming?"

"Yes, and to be honest, that is the fly in the ointment," Sally said. "Mr. Abernathy will only pay for them when they are delivered to the procurement center. That means we'll have to drive three thousand head to Sorento, where we will deliver them to Cephus Malone."

"I thought you said Colin Abernathy. Who is Cephus Malone?"

"Malone works for Abernathy."

"I see. And where is Sorento?"

"It's in Wyoming Territory, near the town of Laramie."

"Whoa, that's almost five hundred miles. You are proposing that we drive three thousand head five hundred miles? Sally, darlin', I know you mean well, but think about it. It would take us a month to get there, and you say that it is just a fly in the ointment. That's a pretty big fly, don't you think?"

"It is, I suppose," Sally said. "But when you think about it, we will have a pretty big fly swat." Sally smiled sweetly at her husband.

"What do you mean, we'll have a pretty big fly swat?"

"Mr. Abernathy is paying thirty-five dollars a head at delivery."

"Thirty-five dollars a head?" Smoke said in surprise. "Why, that's . . ."

"That's one hundred and five thousand dollars," Sally said, finishing Smoke's sentence.

Pearlie dropped his fork and stared across the table at Sally. Cal laughed out loud.

"Pearlie, that's the first time I ever seen anything stop you eatin' in mid-chew," Cal said.

"Miz Sally, did you . . ." Pearlie began, then, remembering that his mouth was full, he finished chewing and swallowed before he returned to his question. "Did you just say one hunnert'n'five thousand dollars?"

"I did say that," Sally said. She smiled at Smoke. "That's why I was able to answer your question as to how much it would cost us to lose three thousand head."

"Lord, I've never seen that much money. I ain't never even heard of that much money," Cal said.

"You haven't said anything, Smoke," Sally said. She took a sip of coffee and stared at her husband over the rim of the cup. "What's the matter? Has the cat got your tongue?"

"That's a lot of money," Smoke said. "And you are right, that is one big fly swat. Something like that would be worth going all the way to Sorento."

"Smoke, do you really think we can drive that many cows all the way to Sorento?" Pearlie asked.

"Looks like we don't have any choice," Smoke said, smiling at Sally. "The boss has spoken."

"Lord, just us?" Cal asked.

Smoke chuckled. "What's the matter, Cal? Don't you think we can do it?"

"I—I reckon so, if you say we can," Cal said, though it was obvious he was unconvinced.

Smoke laughed again. "Don't worry, we'll get some men to help us: drovers, a blacksmith, a cook."

"You won't need a cook," Sally said.

"No cook? Miz Sally, you don't aim for us to make a

drive like that on nothin' but beef jerky, do you?" Pearlie asked.

"No, I expect you to make the drive on bacon and beans, biscuits and cornbread, ham and fried potatoes, some roast beef, steak from time to time, apple pie, and . . . maybe a few bear claws."

"Lord a'mercy, you're goin' with us?"

"No," Smoke said.

"Yes," Sally said at the same time.

"Sally, this isn't some picnic in the country," Smoke said. "I'm not going to let you go."

Sally stared at Smoke with her eyes flashing. "Smoke Jensen. Did you just say what I thought you said? Did you say you aren't going to *let* me go?"

"I, uh . . ." Smoke began, but he stammered to a stop in mid-sentence.

"Cal, if you would be so kind as to hitch up the team, I'll take a wagon into town and pick up all the possibles we're going to need for the drive," Sally said.

Cal looked at Smoke.

Smoke smiled, and shook his head. "Well, do what the lady says," he said. "Maybe a few bear claws would taste good out on the trail."

"Yes, sir!" Cal said with pleasure.

"I'll help you with the team," Pearlie said, following Cal outside.

"I thought you might see it my way," Sally said after the two young men were gone.

"I haven't seen it your way," Smoke said.

"Oh? Kirby Jensen, are you telling me you are going to stop me from going?"

Sally had used Smoke's real name, a sign that she meant business.

"No, hold on now," Smoke said, raising his hands in defense. "I said I haven't seen it your way. I didn't say you weren't going."

Sally smiled. "I didn't think you would actually try to stop me."

"I won't do that," Smoke said. "But if there comes a gully-gusher and you're trying to drive the chuck wagon hub-deep through water and mud, I don't want to hear the slightest complaint from you."

Sally leaned into Smoke and looked flirtatiously into his eyes.

"Why, Smoke, darling," she said. "Do I ever complain?"

GREAT BOOKS,
GREAT SAVINGS!

When You Visit Our Website:
www.kensingtonbooks.com
You Can Save Money Off The Retail Price
Of Any Book You Purchase!

- **All Your Favorite Kensington Authors**
- **New Releases & Timeless Classics**
- **Overnight Shipping Available**
- **eBooks Available For Many Titles**
- **All Major Credit Cards Accepted**

Visit Us Today To Start Saving!
www.kensingtonbooks.com

All Orders Are Subject To Availability.
Shipping and Handling Charges Apply.
Offers and Prices Subject To Change Without Notice.

THE EAGLES SERIES BY
WILLIAM W. JOHNSTONE

__Eyes of Eagles
   0-7860-1364-8   **$5.99**US/**$7.99**CAN

__Dreams of Eagles
   0-7860-6086-6   **$5.99**US/**$7.99**CAN

__Talons of Eagles
   0-7860-0249-2   **$5.99**US/**$6.99**CAN

__Scream of Eagles
   0-7860-0447-9   **$5.99**US/**$7.50**CAN

__Rage of Eagles
   0-7860-0507-6   **$5.99**US/**$7.99**CAN

__Song of Eagles
   0-7860-1012-6   **$5.99**US/**$7.99**CAN

__Cry of Eagles
   0-7860-1024-X   **$5.99**US/**$7.99**CAN

__Blood of Eagles
   0-7860-1106-8   **$5.99**US/**$7.99**CAN

Available Wherever Books Are Sold!

Visit our website at **www.kensingtonbooks.com**